NESTING HABITS OF FLIGHTLESS BIRDS

STORIES

CHRIS HAVEN

TP

TAILWINDS PRESS

Tailwinds Press
P.O. Box 2283, Radio City Station
New York, NY 10101-2283
www.tailwindspress.com

Published in the United States of America
ISBN: 978-1-7328480-6-1
1st ed. 2020

Certainly she dreams often of escape, of reversing
That process by which she came to be here, leaving
As an ordinary emissary carrying her own story,
Sacred news from the reality of artifice,
Out into the brilliant white mystery
Of the truthful world.

"For the Wren Trapped in a Cathedral"
Pattiann Rogers

Nesting Habits of Flightless Birds

Contents

Spare Room

When Mother cleaned, we all felt the guilt.

Years ago, in our house, a woman died. This happened before we moved in, and the agent told us because he was afraid we'd find out anyway. The woman had been murdered. As young girls the three of us should have been frightened, but we were not. The woman had been killed by someone who had loved her once. That person would never murder us, would never love us. We were safe. Looking back, I think I simply must not have believed that love could do something like that.

My older sister speculated that we were spared because mother took the weight of it all on herself.

It was the spare room where it happened—though as I think about the floor plan, this should have been the master bedroom. Mother must have arranged the house to keep contained what that room held. Father never complained, never said a word about the house to the day he died.

Mother cleaned the room differently than she did the other rooms. She used nothing perfumed, no lemon aftereffects, just Borax and other powders. So abrasive it took the stain off the wood. The thin grain of the ash paled under her work. Even as the wood began to splinter, she held to the routine. Every Sunday after the message she would clean on her hands and knees, in the same posture with which she prayed for her own forgiveness.

The walls of the room faded and turned dull. Mother had covered the one small window, but after months of cleaning, the dullness took on at all hours an incandescence, like drying bone under the moon.

We were cautious when we passed the doorway. I knew of ghosts and had the same superstitions as other children. As much as I tried, through closed eyes and open, I could not conjure one. Only once did I feel a presence in there when I sneaked into what I believed to be the empty room, but it was only my mother, there at an unexpected time, sitting on the bed. I had never known her to spend time in the room without cleaning, without attempting to remove something she thought shouldn't be there.

Years later, arranged on her own deathbed, Mother asked us if we were still cleaning the room. She had never asked us to do this as part of our chores, and frankly in the time of her illness, when we had taken over the other work of the house, no one had mentioned the spare room. It had become so much a part of our mother that we no longer considered it a part of the house. I did not tell her we had ignored this task she had set upon herself. Instead, I finally asked Mother why she had cleaned that room so intently over the years.

"It was that woman who lived here before," Mother said.

"Who was she?" I asked. "Did you know her?"

"No," she said. "But every week, she would die that terrible death over again. Every Sunday, it started all over again."

"You were cleaning her blood?"

Mother shook her head. "There was no blood. It was the guilt. It covered the room."

We had all felt the guilt. "But she was murdered," I said. "Why would she feel guilt?"

"We all feel the guilt," Mother said. "It has nothing to do with the blood."

I said no more because I was worried that I was losing a buffer to the inheritance that waited behind that door. As if reading my thoughts, Mother spoke for the last time.

"Don't worry, child," the shake in her voice already a memory. "We don't choose what haunts us."

Assisted Living

At an intersection Jules passed every day, an old man was leaning against the post of a sign that said "Left Turn Only," with not one but two arrows pointing decisively left, into thin air. Jules tapped the steering wheel of his two-year-old Infiniti, leased with the hope that it would lend his buyers confidence to see their real estate agent in a luxury car, presumably not desperate to make a sale. "Come on," he said to the light, stubbornly red on all sides, letting no traffic through. Another glance at the man caught him staring into Jules's tinted window, an unmistakable jutted thumb directed solely at Jules.

Don't pick up hitchhikers, thought Jules. He tried to lock his eyes forward, but could still feel the eyes of the man boring through his window. *Don't sleep with your sister, don't eat human flesh, and don't pick up hitchhikers.* "Rules to live by," he said aloud, but immediately regretted it because the man seemed to bend his head forward, as if Jules were speaking to him.

It wasn't unusual for Jules to see someone standing by the road in Houston in the year 2000, the space-age-sounding year that in spite of its promise still found people wandering around on the ground. Even in heat like this, every day on two separate corners he passed what looked like homeless people selling the newspaper; twice a year blue-shirted firemen from the nearby station held out their boots for donations so they could trot out that oversized check on the telethon; another man up north sat on a plastic cooler selling roses; Jules had even seen junior high cheerleaders with their pompoms, panhandling for money to go to camp. But this old guy didn't seem to be begging. He wore a lime-green collared sport shirt and brown Sansabelt pants, freshly laundered. His skin looked clean, ruddy—not the earthy tan of the Caucasian homeless. The only reason for concern: a patchwork of gauzy, illogical bandages scattered along his left arm.

Jules's hesitation about picking up strangers along the road ran deep. He'd grown up in a prison town, where signs warned: "Hitchhikers May Be Escaping Inmates." It caused him even now to look with suspicion on anyone without access to a car. Still, if the light had not turned, Jules felt he would have been forced to at least acknowledge the man, whose gaze had turned into the most penetrating of questions. Relieved, Jules followed the momentum of traffic. But in checking his rearview mirror, Jules thought he saw the man swoon forward and almost fall.

What if this guy really needed help? Jules had an appointment to show a house to a young couple; he knew they couldn't afford it, but still he had to keep up his contacts. He checked the dashboard clock—if he drove straight there, he'd still have half an hour to kill before the couple arrived. He turned onto the access road of the highway, but he couldn't stop thinking about the old man, faltering in the ninety-degree heat. The temperature indicator inside the Infiniti read a comfortable *72 deg F*. The draft from the vents had blown one patch on each of his forearms frigid—too much air for one man, really. It was excessive, almost shameful. "What the hell," Jules said, and circled into the U-turn lane.

Any thoughts of the man being dangerous were erased when Jules pulled alongside. Up close, the stare that Jules had thought penetrating seemed merely blank. The man still clutched the signpost, but he no longer held out his thumb. Jules flicked on his hazards and stepped out of the car. The man's round, beaverish face seemed not to register Jules's presence at all. "Excuse me," Jules said, not quite knowing what to say. The man's mouth hung open, as if a message were stuck in his throat. Jules put his hand on the man's back, thinking if he could get the man to straighten from his stoop the message might dislodge, like water through an unkinked garden hose.

"Can I help?"

The man's eyes cleared, as if Jules had spoken magic words. "Yes. I think you can." Jules half expected some fairytale plot twist, to be granted a reward, but instead the man retreated into his eyes. No golden eggs from this goose.

In the street, the light had turned green, and the inert Infiniti had caused a minor traffic jam. "Come on," Jules said, rushing to close the deal. "We can talk in the car." The man made no response, but allowed Jules to unbend his fingers from the post and lead him by the elbow to the passenger side of the car. They had to move carefully to dodge the traffic—cars nudged boldly by as if the men were nothing but traffic cones. Jules slammed the door on the man's pants leg once before finally settling him in.

So there it was, Jules thought. He'd picked up his first hitchhiker. Had maybe even forced the guy into it. Sitting in the car, Jules looked the man over. He did not seem like a vagrant, but Jules was no expert on the matter. Even if the man did ask for a handout, he wasn't going to pull out a knife. The real danger was in the responsibility Jules had committed himself to.

Since Jules had no one waiting for him at home, he figured whatever problems this action might present would at most affect only himself. Jules began to feel good about picking this guy up, that he was willing to risk the unknown in order to help a stranger. In the car, the man seemed much larger than he had on the street. Jules sniffed the air—the body odor was noticeable, but not overpowering. Jules had a sudden fear that the man might be incontinent, ruin the upholstery. But what if he did? Wasn't the value of the good deed in direct proportion to the grief it caused? Still, Jules could easily let the man out, deposit him back on the corner. He could make his appointment, carry on with life as usual. But another wave of traffic had gathered behind them, urging them on, so Jules put the car in gear and made the choice to move forward.

Jules was hoping that the man might volunteer some information, a question, point him in a direction. Instead the man gazed out the side window, seemingly content with the ride.

"Gotta be hot standing out there." Jules took quick inventory of the man's appearance. The bandages did not betray a serious injury, and were too high for an IV. He wore no hospital bracelet. "Were you waiting for someone?"

"My son," the man said to the window.

"I see." Jules panicked, afraid he'd made a terrible mistake. "Was he picking you up on that corner?"

The man crossed his hands in his laps in the posture of someone who'd been handcuffed. "He lives in California."

"Is he here visiting?" Jules was already planning where to make the U-turn if he had to return the man to his prearranged meeting place.

"The hound goes to California."

"Right," Jules said, deciding yes, the man was crazy. "A riddle." The messages of the demented that Jules had heard on city streets usually had a religious theme, with references to prophecy and apocalypse with the occasional cameo from Jesus Christ himself.

"The *grey* hound," the man said, impatiently.

"You mean a bus *stop?* You're nowhere near a bus stop, I'm afraid." Jules checked the clock. He still had twenty minutes to make his appointment.

"Sometimes I get confused," the man said. Then he turned to Jules, held his gaze and said, "But I have moments of total clarity."

"Great," Jules said. "How can we tell the difference?"

The man looked away.

Jules felt bad about mocking the guy. "Let me start over. My name is Jules Henry." After waiting what he felt was a polite amount of time for a response, Jules asked, "So what is your name?"

"Otto," he said. "But I don't think that's right."

Jules couldn't help being amused. "Can I *call* you Otto?"

The man seemed to hold this question in front of him, as if considering the freshness of a carton of milk. "If you don't mind being mistaken."

"Otto," Jules said. "Close enough for me."

Jules asked Otto a series of leading questions, with little success. He could not determine where the man lived (he said "inside"), although he mentioned Katy and Linda, two streets miles apart, and parallel to one another. Otto had settled comfortably in his seat and did not betray the slightest inclination towards leaving. Jules himself felt strangely comfortable with Otto, finding it refreshing to finally entertain a passenger in his car who was unsuspicious of him and his motives. More often his clients would keep some distance, which he attributed to their fears of salesmen. Jules thought that some of them even held their purses tighter, or leaned more heavily on their wallets.

Time had come—Jules had to change direction now to make his appointment. It shouldn't take long, Jules figured, and afterwards he could decide what to do with Otto. Besides, where else did the old man have to go?

"How about checking out a house, Otto?"

"Seven," Otto said decisively.

"I'll take that as a yes."

His clients were already at the house, Tammy waiting in the car while Tony knelt in his chinos inspecting the foundation for cracks. Tony didn't know the first thing about foundations, but it gave him something important to do that helped show his young wife that he was capable. Jules had learned a lot about the two over the past few weeks. Tony's background was a little poorer than Tammy's, and she was just a little too pretty for him.

Looking at these larger houses was part of a ruse that afflicted their whole marriage, Jules surmised, a ruse that would eventually crumble around Tony's ankles. The life Jules had imagined for Tony and Tammy stood as just one example of a marriage in which Jules wanted no part, more evidence in favor of living alone.

When Tammy saw Jules's car, she walked over and waited for Jules to open his door. "Tony's distracted as usual," she said, putting her hand on his Infiniti. Jules was uncomfortable with the tension he felt around Tammy. Her right cheekbone raised slightly higher than the other when she smiled, suggesting a wink. He felt she was flirting, but with his car and not himself.

Before Jules could open the passenger door, Otto was already out, suddenly purposeful, as if he had arrived at his own home.

"Oh—" Tammy said, cut short. "Guess this one's in demand," she said, a note of competition in her voice.

"No, no. He's not a buyer. This is . . ."

"My son," Otto said, grabbing Tammy's hand from her side, shaking it vigorously.

Tony joined them grinning, circles of grass stains on the knees of his chinos. "Nice to meet you, Mr. Henry. Your son has been quite a help to us."

"Otto isn't my father," Jules said, and in response to the confusion on their faces added, "He's my grandfather."

Why Jules decided to promote Otto from slightly demented stranger to grandfather he didn't know. But as soon as Jules said it, he liked the idea of adopting this man. Jules felt Otto needed him. Not like Tony and Tammy or any of his clients thought they needed him, but in a more basic, vital way. Who knows what might have happened to him on that busy intersection? Jules allowed himself to think he had saved Otto's life.

Jules unlocked the door to the five-bedroom Cape Cod. Normally he would have walked Tony and Tammy through the house, highlighting the recent maintenance, age of the appliances, condition of the roof. But this time he let them find their own way, instead focusing his attention on Otto.

"Ever been in a house like this, Otto?"

Otto studied the vaulted ceiling. "Yes," he said. "I've been in this one."

Jules started. Was this one of Otto's moments of clarity? Had he found the man's home? "No kidding? When?"

"Today," he said and smiled.

"Good one," Jules said. Maybe Otto was understanding more than Jules had thought. "This deal will run about a quarter mil," Jules said. Behind his hand he whispered, "Tony will get approved at one-eighty max."

Otto nodded. "Everybody needs approval."

Tony and Tammy clambered down the stairs, beaming. "Oh Jules," Tammy said. "You've outdone yourself." From Tammy, this could have meant anything. She "loved" every house she saw. Hers was an indecipherable ranking system that ran from "cute" to "darling." But Tony, usually full of energy, looked concerned. He asked Jules about deed restrictions, as usual.

"In your packet," Jules said. "Homeowner's dues are forty, surveillance another fifty."

He left the couple whispering to each other, rifling through papers, paying no attention to the house at all. Papers—the separation between the house and the dream.

Some people had a fear of the dotted line. Even to the sweetest deal some people couldn't sign their name. Some people didn't believe they deserved happiness.

"Come on Otto, let's check out the upstairs." Inadvertently, Jules slapped his leg, as if calling a dog. He felt immediately ashamed.

Upstairs, Jules stepped onto a balcony that overlooked the backyard. He leaned against the railing and imagined what Tony and Tammy must be thinking. Otto joined him, warily peeking over the balcony.

"They've probably got this place all outfitted: barbecue, swingset, happy kids. The works," Jules said. "But they don't get it. A house is a structure, you know what I mean?"

"Don't dwell in the future," Otto said, backing away from the railing.

"Exactly," Jules said. "I don't mind showing dream houses. No sales, but I figure everybody needs a dream house, a place to go. I've seen people actually get their dream house. But it's never the same. Lot of times they end up selling it right back. The only place for a dream house is in your imagination. Because a dream can't fit into a structure. That, my friend, is why I rent."

Jules turned, but Otto was not on the balcony. "What about you, Otto? How about if you buy this house? I could cut you a killer deal. Otto?"

Jules found him inside the bedroom, pants at his thighs, peeing in a corner.

"Holy—" Jules lunged toward Otto, but held back. The pouch of Otto's shorts hung limp from the waistband, which clung tightly across the loose flesh of his rear end. "Otto!"

Otto finished, pulled up his pants. When he saw Jules,

Otto's face screwed up like an infant's, tears squirting nickel stains onto his shirt.

The puddle was surprisingly small, disappearing quickly into a dark stain. Jules jerked his head around the empty room, finding nothing to clean the mess. Another couple of minutes and it would soak into the pad. Almost as soon as he realized his helplessness, Jules decided he didn't care. What was one little corner of carpet?

"Jules?" Tony called from the bottom of the stairs, hesitantly climbing the steps.

"Yes," Jules said, then loudly called, "No—you stay there. I'll come down." Jules left the balcony doors open to dissipate the smell. Holding Otto's arm to his body like a football, Jules led him down the stairs.

"We really appreciate your time today," Tony said. "I know we've been a bother . . . "

"No bother," Jules said.

"Don't bother," Otto said, yanking his arm back.

Tony and Tammy both smiled politely as Otto opened the front door. "Will you be around later?" Tony asked Jules.

"Voice mail," Jules said, leading them out the door as quickly as possible, before the smell could hit them. "I'm always around."

Tammy smiled her goodbye to Jules with that chin-down, winking smile that Jules figured had worked on a line of men from her father to her teachers, boyfriends, mechanics, clerks, straight through to her husband. Yes, Jules admitted, probably it even worked on him.

Otto, who had stopped crying, arrested Tony before he got to his car. He held him by the shoulders as if explaining a rule to a child. "Make it work."

Tony smiled nervously before Otto released him. Jules wondered what Tony was thinking. Probably thought Otto was giving Jules a message that meant something. About buying a house. About Tony's marriage, maybe. When Otto turned away Jules noticed Otto's shirttail peeking out of his fly. Jules laughed silently. Make it work—the old man could've just meant his zipper. *Tony,* thought Jules. *Poor bastard.*

In the car, Otto sniffled. "It's okay. Don't worry," Jules said. "Carpet cleaners—it'll be like new." After a showing Jules would usually check his messages, do the follow-ups. But he felt guilty for putting Otto in a position where he could embarrass himself. Jules decided he should make it up to Otto.

"You ever have a dream house, Otto? Let me show you the ones I have." Jules drove by his area listings, reciting the floor plans from memory. What size family should occupy, potential for appreciation, resale value.

Outside the first house—a two-bedroom split-level— Otto said, "Too close to the highway."

"Come on Otto, what would it take for me to put you in this house? I've gotta make you a sale."

Jules drove by about twenty of the homes on his list, and pitched the rest from his listings book. Otto always countered, sometimes dead-on, other times nonsensical: "Too much house," or "Not enough yard," or "The easement's too wide."

"You're smart to be careful. When you buy a house, you don't buy bricks and wood. You buy a concept," Jules said, tapping his temple. "A house isn't a financial investment, but the beginning of a relationship."

Otto fidgeted, adjusted the air conditioning vent.

"You buy that?" Otto didn't respond, and Jules thought he looked skeptical. "Me, either," Jules said. "Hard to see having a relationship with a house. I guess people are the only ones who can have relationships."

"Your ship has come in," Otto said.

"What'll it be, Otto? At least pick a favorite. Which one did you like best?"

Otto paused, as if considering the question. "This one," he said, stroking the leather interior.

"Which? The car?" Jules nodded. "I should have guessed—you're a mobile kind of guy. Like me."

Then, from a remote place in the car, a grumbling danced into Jules's ears. Jules clicked off the air conditioner to listen, afraid something might be wrong with the car. When the grumbling sounded a second time, Jules pinpointed its origin: Otto's belly.

"Feed the kitty," Otto said.

Jules had meant to drive to a nice, sit-down restaurant, but when Otto recognized a Wendy's sign he could not be talked out of it. At the drive-through Otto waited for the voice in the speaker, then leaned over Jules's lap and ordered: "Spicy Chicken Sandwich, Biggie Fries and a Biggie Drink." With all the holes in Otto's memory, Jules was amazed at how these fast-food terms had taken hold.

When it came time to pay, Otto calmly passed his wallet to Jules. The sight of such a common object as a wallet took Jules by surprise. It was like finding a collar buried beneath the fur of a dog you'd thought was a stray. The wallet was a sign that Otto had a tangible identity, even if to Otto himself that identity remained elusive. Jules unfolded the wallet, found a driver's license. *Otto Kightling.* In the photo, he was wearing the same green shirt, as if the picture had been taken that day. Jules shook his head. "Damn thing's current."

"Pass the fries," Otto said.

Jules paid with his own money and used his cell phone to call information. He'd only had the phone a short time, and this was the first time he'd used the phone for anything resembling an emergency. When the salesman had sold Jules the phone he'd pitched a list of imagined dangers—blowouts, carjackings, overturned semis— conjuring doom that awaited you when you were away from home. Mobility came with a price, apparently, but at no time did the salesman mention disoriented old men eating chicken sandwiches in your car. Jules dialed. "What do you know, Otto? You're in the book." The woman who answered identified herself as Linda, Otto's daughter. Mystery solved. "Linda. 701 Katy. Got it."

Otto munched on his fries, having already dispatched the sandwich. "We've got to get you home now, old boy," Jules said. "You're finally going home."

Otto made no response, but stopped eating. His face tightened, and his color went gray. Why wouldn't he want to go home? Maybe Linda didn't treat Otto very well. He didn't seem to be abused, not physically anyway, but who could tell? Jules started to panic. He stopped the car. Jules knew he couldn't just take Otto home to live with him, but maybe he could let him sleep on the couch, until they figured something out. Just as Jules was about to ask Otto what he thought of the idea, Otto burped.

"Spicy," he said, exhaling. Otto sipped his drink, and the color returned to his face. Then Otto looked around, as if noticing something for the first time. "We're not moving," he said.

"Are you ready to go home?" Jules asked.

"We should be moving."

Jules started the car, headed toward Otto's house. *Just as well,* Jules thought, feeling foolish. *Can't even recognize a little gas attack.*

Otto's house looked solid enough—A-frame, all wood. In an older neighborhood, but well-kept. Still, it lay outside the desirable center loop of the city. "Convert that carport into a garage, and plop this house down six miles from here, you'd add thirty-five K to the bottom line."

"Houses don't plop," Otto said.

"Hard to argue with that," Jules said, stopping the car. "So this is it?" Jules hoped Otto would show some recognition of the house, but all he said was, "I have a son in California."

"California?" For a moment, Jules thought it possible—to drive away and try to find that son. California sounded nice. Jules had heard the ocean breezes made it cool, even in the summer.

Otto leaned over, whispered, "As soon as I remember his name, I'm going out to see him."

"If this were a movie," Jules said, "You and I would go to California. Be a great buddy picture."

"I don't think this is a movie," Otto said. "Is it?"

What else could Jules do? He walked Otto to the door.

Linda looked to be nearly as old as Otto, deep, honest lines marking her face. Jules noticed a faint smell of cigarette smoke mixed with bath powder. The rich earth tones of the carpet and dark wood paneling—twenty years out of style—made the house seem close, like heavy hands of air squeezed him on all sides. Though it was late in the evening, Linda was dressed, her walking shoes on, purse on the table. Ready to act, if asked. When she saw Jules and Otto, she seemed interested, but not overly concerned. "How far did he make it?"

"Picked him up just off 290, close to the loop."

Linda shook her head. "He's never made it that far before," she said. "But he always finds his way back home."

She regarded Otto as if he were her own child, a toddler who, even though mischievous, managed to be lovable in spite of his misbehavior. Otto retrieved an empty coffee cup from the kitchen shelf and sat expectantly at the table. Linda poured his coffee, completing what Jules thought must serve as Otto's returning home ritual. The cup read, *World's #1 Dad.*

"He mentioned something about a son in California," Jules said.

"Did he?" she said. "News to me. He's always wanted a son, though. No telling what kind of life he lives in his head. Maybe it's better . . . "

But Jules wasn't ready to dismiss Otto so easily. Maybe he *did* have a son, one she didn't know about. Jules wanted Linda to know that he was still on Otto's side. "Seems risky," Jules said, trying to put a note of disapproval in his voice. "Counting on this city to bring him back."

"I know," she said, apparently unoffended. "I've made arrangements. It's not a home—they call it assisted living."

"I've heard of it," Jules said. They used to call them nursing homes; now, people found this term easier to stomach. Before, he'd always thought of places like that as a boost to business, recycling people's homes back into the market. But today he wanted to tell Linda that she shouldn't abandon her father like that. Otto deserved better.

"What about those bandages on his arm?" Jules asked suspiciously.

"He likes to play in the medicine cabinet," she shrugged. "I've taken out everything that might hurt him." Linda watched Otto sip his coffee. "I hope he wasn't a problem. Can I pay you?"

"Absolutely not," Jules said, indignant, then felt Otto's wallet bulging in his pocket. "Here," Jules offered, red-faced. "I, uh, needed it for his ID. Go ahead and check it."

Linda took the wallet, but before she could open it Otto poured the contents of his coffee cup onto the kitchen table. The steaming liquid inched its way towards the edge of the table. Linda ran for a towel and mopped up the spill before it hit the floor.

"Cleaning up," Otto said, delighted.

"I suppose I should go," Jules said, seeing there was nothing he could do here. He patted Otto on the back. "If I can help . . . " he said, and gave Linda his card.

She put the towel down. "Real estate?" Linda said. "Daddy was an agent, you know."

"No kidding?" Jules looked at Otto, who flashed a conspiratorial look.

"Forty years," she said. "No retirement, of course."

"I hear you," Jules said. "Health insurance?"

"No, no. That makes it hard . . . " Her voice trailed off, then she said, "I figure he sold nearly a thousand homes."

Otto looked up from the table. "I've been in his home," he said secretively.

Linda smiled at her father. "That's nice."

In the ensuing silence, Jules realized that he had to

leave right then. No matter what he'd thought earlier, he knew now that he wouldn't be the one to rescue this man. "Otto, it's been a pleasure," Jules said. "Sorry we couldn't make a deal."

"I've been in your home," Otto said.

"Yes," Jules said, his foot in the door, ready to escape. "And you're welcome there anytime."

On his way home Jules received a page from Tony. Their pre-approval had come through, and they were ready to make an offer of 220. Jules couldn't believe it—the offer was low, but he was sure it would fly. Tony had done it. He'd put Tammy in her dream home. *Poor bastard,* Jules thought again, imagining the avalanche of new promises Tony would always be struggling to fulfill.

As Jules gathered the fast food trash from the passenger seat of his car and walked to his apartment, he experienced the familiar pull of home, the weariness in the body that came from letting down the defenses of the day. When he closed the door behind him the plate on the knob, loose for months now, rattled comfortably against his hand. He flipped the light switch, but only the ceiling fan came on—he must have turned off the bulb at the cord that morning. Even though the room was pitch dark, Jules decided not to turn on the light. His apartment stretched before him, hidden. The fan churned the air, steamy from the day's heat. Jules tried to walk the wide middle path from his living room to the kitchen. How hard could it be? He took a few tentative steps forward, and the corner of something sharp dug into his shoulder. Unable to place what he had bumped into, Jules grabbed his shoulder and backed away, his heart pounding, for a second wondering if he was in the right apartment. Even after he recognized the object as his television stand, and though he knew it was ridiculous, Jules had the unmistakable feeling that he was being watched. Tested. He put his hands out and groped his way along the wall. In the dark, his apartment seemed larger than he remembered, and he could not gauge his steps correctly. Jules staggered to the kitchen, stumbling once over a dining room chair, and, with the help of the blue glow from the numbers *3:24* on the microwave clock—not even close to the right time—he finally put Otto's trash in the wastebasket. On his way out of the kitchen, Jules brushed his hand on the bottom frame of a small mirror. He felt it topple and tried to catch it, but it fell to the floor, shattering. He knew he should just turn the light on, clean up the mess. What a stupid way to hurt yourself. But Jules decided it was worth the risk. He had to keep trying. *I can do this,* he thought. *I can find my way.* This was *his* home, these were *his* things. He did not need assistance. There was an order here—he just had to uncover it. Glass crunched under his feet as he moved forward. *This is a test,* he thought, and he knew then that all anyone could hope to do in the world was respond somehow, even if the response made no sense.

The Lucky Ones

The Club

After his thirtieth birthday, George joined a health club because everyone asked him how it felt to be thirty. He didn't know because he didn't feel any older, only fatter. He decided to recapture his youth and his waistline. George loves jogging on the track at the club. It is nicely padded and the surface is smooth and even—it takes him exactly sixty-eight strides to go around once. Every stride gets him closer to where he wants to be. If he just knew the right numbers, the right formula, everything would be all right.

The people at the club stuff their bodies into polyester tights, but George knows that the bulges are more than just fat—they are getting rid of all the junk in their lives, like you would at a garage sale. Lots of things are stuffed into those tights: the toys you had as a child, outgrown clothes, a broken lawnmower, a moth-eaten quilt, a jigsaw puzzle, a pair of boots, your dead father's tools, and all those other goddamned things you've done wrong. If you run hard enough, they will all disappear. George is precise with every step he takes, always remembering, always frightened.

Lovers

George and Susan were once lovers. Before marriage, before they knew their friends Jerry and Ellie, before they had couple friends at all, they didn't need anyone else. Jerry asks George about children.

"It's her. She won't stop taking the pill."

"What's the problem? Is she scared?"

"She won't talk about it. Sometimes I'm insulted, but most of the time, I just feel like she knows more than I do."

Counseling

It is Jerry's idea; he mentions it to George. Jerry is going bald, and he flaunts it. He gets his hair cut shorter than it should be, to show everyone he doesn't care. Jerry tells George about a marriage counselor. "He saved my own marriage."

George is willing to try, but he is skeptical. Just as his own eye doctor tells him he can't correct his vision back to 20/20, a counselor could never know the depth of their problem.

Jerry insists this will be different. "It just took a couple of weeks. It all came together when he told us a story. It was about a couple who was completely happy. Completely in love. The real thing, they both thought. Then one day, the guy asks the wife if she remembers the first time they met. She tells him when she thought it was, then he tells her that no, he saw her months before, in a restaurant. She was leaving just as he was being seated. He knew as soon as he saw her that she was his dream girl. He couldn't believe his luck when they finally met. Then, to actually marry your dream girl—he was the luckiest guy alive. Turns out she tells him she was never at that restaurant. Never even heard of it."

George whistles.

Jerry nods. "It's all about expectations."

"So this guy put their marriage back together?"

"No, it was too late for them. The point is, it's not too late for you."

The Helpful Neighbor

George finds it hard to believe, but encouraging, that Susan has agreed to do this. Jerry's wife, Ellie, is responsible. Ellie's upper lip curls around her teeth in a way George considers suspicious. She leans toward you when she speaks, as if her feet are nailed to the floor, and treats your ear as if it were a microphone. She even looks at your ear while she's speaking. George knows this is the way Ellie must have talked Susan into counseling. It's possible Ellie knows Susan now better than he knew her when they first met. Anything is possible.

Symptoms

The doctor is a small man, younger than George expects. He uses a small tape recorder, and moves the microphone toward them like a reporter.

"Why did you decide it was time to get help?"

George glances at Susan. "I guess it's like when you have a toothache, but don't want to go to the dentist. You put it off and put it off until one day, you just have to go. You have no choice."

Susan and George exchange looks. She looks surprised, but George can't tell in what way.

"You go because the tooth hurts?" the doctor asks.

"That's right," George says.

"No," Susan says.

George looks at his wife. He always listens to her, and tries very hard to understand her, though her moods often overwhelm him. He has learned that he cannot rely on merely what she says, but on every clue he can get from all of his senses: the spread of her lips when she speaks, the depression of her hand when they touch, the taste of her mouth when they kiss. He feels like a deep-space astronomer, dealing with an instrument that works only in theory, with data billions of years old.

"No," he says. "She's right. You learn to live with the everyday pain. But one day the tooth hurts so much, you can't even eat."

"Not even soup," Susan says.

"Nope, not even soup," says George. "You get hungry."

The doctor says, "And when you go to the dentist, does he pull the tooth or try to save it?"

"Whatever it takes to eat again," Susan says.

"Whatever it takes," agrees George.

The Dividing Point

The doctor, with the recorder running, says, "Tell me. For each of you, what was the very worst point? The one time you knew that you couldn't take it anymore."

George sits back in his seat. "There *was* a low point." He looks at Susan.

Susan nods. "The autumnal equinox."

"That's right. It was awfully hot outside, not like fall at all. She was very upset. She said it was the first day of fall, but it still felt like summer."

"It was so hot. There wasn't any difference at all."

George turns to the doctor. "I told her you aren't supposed to feel the difference the first day. I told her that going from summer to fall was more of a gradual thing."

"If you can't depend on the first day of fall, what can you depend on?"

"Just because the calendar says it's the first day of fall doesn't mean that day has to *act* like fall. I told her, there have to be divisions. There has to be a time, however arbitrary, that one thing ends so another can begin."

Susan stares at the wall. "And then I started crying . . ."

George looks at his feet. "She was crying so hard, and I couldn't stop her."

Homework

The doctor assigns homework. He liked the metaphor about the dentist, so he asks George and Susan to make up their own metaphors about the marriage.

George is good at word games. He works crossword puzzles religiously. He knows that the clue *Word of woe* is ALAS or ALACK, *King of comedy* is ALAN, *Auction ending* is EER, *King toppers* is never CROWNS but ACES, and *Nothing* is very often LOVE.

"I think this whole thing is stupid," Susan says.

"Come on, let's give it a try." George knows he is too excited, but he can't help himself. "It might be fun."

Susan looks at him with what George thinks could be pity, but George is used to the look. "Oh, all right."

"Good." George pats the arm of his chair. "I've thought of one. Our marriage was like we were on the rooftop of a tall building, and there was this other building that we had to jump to. The jump was our marriage. But we didn't jump far enough, and we had to hold onto the roof of that other building by our fingertips."

"For eleven years?" Susan says.

"Well . . ."

"Eleven years we were hanging by our fingertips? That's not right."

"Why not?"

Susan slumps as if she's very tired. "We couldn't have been hanging from a building for eleven years. Whatever it was, I know our marriage hasn't been eleven years of sheer terror. It hasn't even been impending doom."

The Lucky Ones

George tries again, the next night. "I've got another one. Our marriage was like we were on top of this really tall tower and we jumped off."

"We jumped." George can see Susan showing interest in spite of herself. "Why did we jump?"

"The jump was our marriage. We did it together. We fell and fell . . ."

"For eleven years."

"For eleven years, and then we hit the ground."

"That's stupid. Why would anyone jump off a tower?" Susan asks.

"We *had* to jump. The jump was our marriage. We both wanted to, didn't we?" George needs Susan to give him the right answer.

"Yes, we both wanted to, but I don't know."

Relieved, George says, "Let me finish. We could've jumped off a higher tower, see? We could've *built* a higher tower."

"So high it would have lasted us the rest of our lives?"

George considers this for a moment. "Yes, people do that. The lucky ones with marriages that last do. Only they die *before* they hit bottom."

George is proud of this, but Susan is frowning.

"I don't think that's right, about our marriage being a tower."

"It's not the tower, it's the jump *from* the tower."

"Whatever, that's not right either. It's not right because falling is scary. It's a wicked, intense excitement. If there's one thing we haven't had in our marriage, it is intense excitement."

Faith

"It seems to me, George, that all your metaphors so far seem to involve falling."

Susan leans forward in her chair, secretive. "Yes, Doctor. George has always believed that marriage is a sort of epic adventure."

"Well, not an epic adventure," George says. "But certainly a leap of faith. I still believe that."

The Hobby

George understands falling and flight very well, ever since he started hang-gliding. He got the idea from a commercial he saw while he was watching a football game on television. Sometimes after sitting for a long time, his chest would hurt every time he took a breath. He would get dizzy and claustrophobic, feeling as if the air around him was thickening. After he stood and stretched for a moment he would be fine, but he always vowed to change his life after these spells, feeling sure his heart was weak. He would diet for a while, or exercise, until the time he saw the commercial and decided he should try hang-gliding. He needed that high-altitude air rushing in his face and through his lungs. He thought it would clean his body.

It works wonders for him. He spends Saturdays leaping into the sky, splitting the world in two with the point of the glider, leaving the sky quivering on the ground below him. It doesn't cure his attacks, but when he's in the air, he knows exactly who he is. He defies death every time he runs off a cliff with the glider. He tells Jerry, "That glider makes me believe in myself, even if it's just for a few minutes."

The Circus

"Okay, how about this one?" George says. "Our marriage was like a high-wire act, performed without a net."

"A high-wire act?" Susan asks. George knows she loves the circus.

"Yes, a tightrope. We were walking on a tightrope, without a net, in a great big circus. The circus was our life."

"But if we were the high-wire act, we couldn't see the circus."

"So the circus was the world outside us, the life we were missing. Then all of a sudden, we slip, and hit the ground."

Susan stands up. "Listen. Where do you come off with all this hitting the ground stuff? Do you think we're at a point of sudden realization? Enlightenment? We haven't learned anything, have we George?"

"No, we haven't."

"Then did it kill us?" Susan steps back. "We're not dead, George. Are we dead?"

"No, we're not. I guess we're not."

Susan

Susan did use to love the circus. Whenever she went she would eat funnel cake and cotton candy. Her favorites were the clowns. She liked to imagine that the long whirls of their pink and green hair were made of cotton candy. She tore off pieces of the candy and let them melt on her tongue when she watched the clowns. Maybe they were made completely of the candy. She cringed when they threw water on each other because she was afraid they would melt away.

But she loved the trick with the little car. The door would open, and clowns would come out and keep coming out until you couldn't believe another one could ever come out but one would and so you had to keep believing in one more clown, just one more, even after the last one came out and the car drove away.

Susan liked the lightness of the circus, because she felt light herself. Sometimes she felt like she might be made of cotton candy too, with too much air that made her seem much larger than she actually was. She was really very tiny. If you made a loud noise, she might collapse like a cake, to her real size. She felt light, so light, but she couldn't explain it to anyone. She tried to tell George once, joking, "My soul has swallowed too much air. I need spiritual burping." But he just stared at her like a blinded animal.

Perpetual Daze

"Okay, I think I've got it. Our marriage was like a ski trip. We started out on top of this really high mountain, going crazy in the dark, with no idea of where we're going. Then all of a sudden, one day, or one day in the dark, after eleven years, wham, we plow into a tree, never knowing what hit us."

"Are we dead?"

"No, no. We're just stunned. We remain in a perpetual daze."

Susan nods. "That's close. That's almost right. But I don't know about the trip part."

"But that's right. I mean, our marriage was like a diversion from real life. We were going on a vacation."

"Yes, that part's right. But a ski trip is too elaborate. We would have to rent the skis and everything, and go to the top of this really God-awful big mountain."

"That's right."

"It sounds like a lot of preparation to me. And if there's one thing our marriage wasn't built on, it's preparation."

The Ski Trip

Susan remembers the ski trip they went on a few years ago. It was a disaster. She had never skied before, so she spent two miserable days in lessons while George skied with Jerry and Ellie. The sky was a thick, murky gray, full of snow that never came. The sun was a bitter, dull half-dollar stuck in the sky, offering no relief from the cold. The runs were mainly covered with artificial snow. When Susan finally felt comfortable enough on her skis to go up the lift, she was afraid of the wind and the swirling snow.

"It's all blowing away," she told George. When she got to the top of the mountain, she was sure that the snow would be gone by the time she got down. She would crash among the rocks and trees. In spite of George's assurances, she refused to go down the slope, and she had to be escorted down in a sled by the ski patrol.

George was furious. He had wanted to be the one to rescue her. When they walked back to the lodge, he took off his stocking cap and began yelling. Susan didn't hear anything he said. He had a crew cut, and steam rose from his head at a terrific rate. Susan imagined there were little animals inside his head, building a fire in George, the great big chimney.

George was still unhappy with her that night. The distance he kept from her in bed seemed to be measured in time and not space. The farther away he was from her, the younger Susan became. They had a fire going, but she was cold all night. George was awakened by her sobbing in the middle of the night. She had thrown her covers off and she was curled up, hugging herself tightly. When he touched her arm she said, "I'm blowing away."

He told her softly that she was dreaming, and pulled her close to him. "My poor baby, blowing away like a little leaf."

Susan pulled back. "No, I was a sand castle. I was crumbling in the wind."

The Game

"Are you sleeping apart?" the doctor asks.

"We tried that for a while," Susan says. "But George couldn't do it."

"That's right. I couldn't sleep. I would doze off for a while, but I'd wake up all twisted, and my hands would be numb."

"I had to come back."

"That's right."

"One of us would leave, then we'd come back."

Susan puts her hands to her face, thinking. She puts her hands down and turns to George. "That's it. That's how it was. I know what it was like."

"Really?"

"It was like the game with the hands. You remember—you put out your right hand, and I put my hand on top of yours. Then you put your left hand on top, and I put my left hand on top of that."

"The hand-sandwich game."

"And now your right hand is at the bottom of the sandwich, so you take it out and put it on top. And I pull my right hand out and put *it* on top. Sometimes the game would get fast, and your hands would get all mixed up. But playing the game, the thing is, you always feel like there are more hands there."

"Yeah."

"Like there is a mountain of hands, strong ones that can do anything. In the stack, your hands are always touching hands, and you feel safe and strong."

"That's it."

"Then one day, after eleven years, we realized that all that was in the stack were our four hands. And we stopped playing the game. Out of embarrassment."

"Embarrassment."

The sky spills orange clouds onto the horizon. George says, "Look out the window. The sun is going down. It looks just like a . . . "

"It's like a sunset." Susan folds her hands neatly in her lap.

Excellent Mother

This lower-middle-class apartment outside the loop in Houston is the nicest place of your own you've lived. It's a well-kept property: lush Bermuda grass, brick accents in the sidewalks, rows of flowers guarding compressors for the air conditioners that run round the clock. The grounds are nice enough that you took pictures and sent them to the in-laws, to demonstrate how well you and Stacy have progressed in the adult stage of life.

Wide parking lots separate the buildings; like everywhere in the city, car is king. In the million-dollar condos that dot the inner loop, garages are often the most prominent feature, relegating the living spaces to the background. The city gives the illusion of distance.

In your apartment, you know the habits of your closest neighbors quite well.

The couple above is better than six hundred pounds between them, and on several nights each month, their affection for each other tests the limits of the support beams in your ceiling. The man's voice is deep, and he enjoys hearing it say to his big wife, "Oh baby." You sometimes imitate that voice into Stacy's ear. She still finds it funny. Sometimes the noise will be too much and Stacy will move to the couch, leaving you to keep watch over the baby, whose crib lines a wall in your room.

Like half of your friends that you left back in Austin, you're a parent now. How that collection of musicians and half-time grad students will make it as parents you often wonder. You feel you're on firmer ground than them, but who knows. Your boy, Charles, is six months old, a good baby with rolls of doughy fat on his legs that are fun to squeeze. He does cry, but sometimes he's so quiet you wonder if he's figured out he's supposed to be alive yet.

The job of caring for your son is both yours and Stacy's, but it's fallen more on your shoulders. The restaurant where Stacy works as a manager transferred her here, and the freelancing that you do can be done from home, so you stay home with the baby. You run a YouTube channel that began by specializing in video instructions for smartphones, but now you'll review most anything. The written instructions that come with the products are either confusing, poor, or simply missing, so you get plenty of subscribers. The checks are coming in for both of you, but because of the moving expenses and old bills, you still live as if you're a couple of years poorer than you really are.

Stacy acts happy with the arrangement, but you know she's torn. If things turn around for you financially, maybe Stacy will quit her job. You suspect she thinks she would be better at raising your son than you, and part of you wants to prove you can do the job.

Stacy gets up at noon and eats breakfast, toast and jelly. She tries to eat as many of her meals at the restaurant as possible, to save money, but lately she's stopped eating with the help. "The other managers don't do it. I think it's because they don't want to seem as poor as they really are. But I miss it. I don't feel like myself."

As she finishes her orange juice, a report comes on about a woman who went to work and left her baby in the backseat of her car all day. You don't have to be told how the story ends—it doesn't take long for the Houston heat to take a life.

"I can't imagine what that child went through," you say.

"I can't imagine what that *mother* went through," Stacy says. "How can she live with that?" Stacy's powers of empathy are far stronger than yours. You can see on her face that she is losing herself, slipping into the tragedy of that other mother's life.

This is the latest in a series of hot car deaths. Last week a stranger went so far as to smash the tinted window of a black Jetta to rescue what turned out to be a Build-A-Bear stuffed teddy, strapped into a backward-facing Britax carseat.

The news vultures show footage of the father returning from work, overlaid with the voices of the woman's coworkers testifying in her favor: "She is very caring. She loved her baby. She's an excellent mother."

"You would never do something like that," you say, trying to snap Stacy out of whatever it is she's doing to herself.

"I don't know. What if I was so tired I couldn't think straight?"

"Not you. This woman next door maybe, I could see that. But not you."

The new neighbors moved in two weeks ago, and they

made the amorous couple above seem like no problem at all. At first things were fine, but then they started yelling at each other in the early morning, easy to hear through the walls. He's a fit, good-looking guy; she's an enormous bleach blonde with a voice that pulls at you like a scab. One night he yells: *You got some and didn't bring me any? Where's mine?* F-bombs ricochet off the walls, from both of them. He's very angry that she has gotten high without him. You and Stacy have discussed calling the police, fearful for the woman's safety. If it comes to blows, frankly, you're more worried for the guy because he's quite a bit smaller.

They have a seven-year-old daughter. You hope she is a deep sleeper.

She's a pretty little brown-haired girl named Claudia who runs wild—in the parking lot, down to the swimming pool, the play area behind the building, and who knows where else. She doesn't look like either one of the parents, and you wonder if the girl is his. You can't imagine him sleeping with this woman, and it's not just her physical appearance. There is nothing attractive about her. Every evening, the mother will belly up to the stockade fence that encloses the front porch, put her hands to her mouth and yell in a smoker's voice, *Clau-die! Clau-die!* The sound grates, echoes through the complex, cutting wood. It goes on long enough that you think you better round up a search party because if Claudia can't hear that chainsaw calling, she must be in real trouble. Just as you're at your most uncomfortable, Claudia comes wandering home, perfectly content. It's in these moments that you imagine the neighbor woman thinks she has done the duty she's been put on this earth to perform, taking time out of her busy day getting high to bring her child back from the grips of the dark.

When it's time for Stacy to leave for work, she holds onto Charles and kisses him all around his neck. She looks into your eyes and whispers, "I don't want to go." You nod, and take Charles from her. If he's eating when Stacy leaves, he doesn't get upset. You prop him up in his bouncy seat and give him his bottle. As Stacy slips out the door her eyes haze over. You give her a kiss and say, "Shh. Honey. You're an excellent mother."

One day you come back from a walk with your boy. You've fastened him into one of those packs where he faces you, rides on your chest. It's supposed to build a bond, but you can't stop thinking about how horribly the instructions had been written. If you'd followed them literally, strapping him in would have strangled the both of you.

When you near your door, you see your neighbors are having a cookout on the front porch. Your lease explicitly says that a barbeque grill is not allowed and is grounds for eviction. Another couple is over, and you hear your neighbor call him little brother. Which is weird because the guy is huge, ripped like a professional wrestler, and tatted up. Wife beater, of course, and mirrored sunglasses. You can quickly see your neighbor is proud of his little brother. They each have baseball gloves on, and they are on the ten-foot strip of grass between the cars and the porches, ripping the ball. Bringing serious heat. The ball rockets into their gloves, echoing like gunshots across the complex.

You wait, your child's legs dangling bare from the

poorly described sling, the baseball whipping five feet from the gate you're supposed to walk in. Surely they will stop and hold the ball to let you and your infant pass. These boneheads don't stop.

Each throw your neighbor makes is intended to show that he measures up to his little brother. Older brother is average-sized, but a guy like that can still throw hard. He even has a baseball hat on. Each toss is a statement. *This is something in life I can control. I can put this ball in your glove and I can put it there hard and precise and with regularity. I can do this all night. I can do it long past the time you lose your interest. I am zoned in, I am all here, but at the same time I'm relaxed. This calms me. It's like I'm getting a massage right now.* Eyes a little sleepy, rolls the neck between throws. Smooth as whiskey. The thunk of the glove. The catch. Still, it's teamwork. The joint purpose. You don't play throw. You play catch.

Their wives watch them from lawn chairs, chomping on illegal hamburgers. The muscled brother has a wife who is Miami Beach beautiful. You wonder what older brother thinks about this. How deep does their competition run?

Claudia is playing with three other children, all older than her, at the side of the apartment. The game is unclear, but she stands in the center of the group, whining. The kids stop to stare at her and she gets louder. This crybaby is used to getting her way. You wish you liked her more so you could feel sorry for her and the lousy situation she's in with these parents of hers, but you don't. She cries more, sits in the dirt. One of the older boys leans down and says something to her, then he offers his hand, lifting her to her feet. She has gotten what she wanted.

You decide to trust the skills of these maniacs and walk on by because they're not stopping their game for anything. You open your gate and the pretty one has her legs crossed in a showy, uncomfortable way. Claudia's mother has never looked up from her sandwich. The sound of the baseball hitting a glove continues its *thunk thunk* well after you've warmed the bottle for your son and released him and yourself from this ridiculous contraption.

That night, hours before your wife gets home—a knock on your door. You're not expecting anyone. The complex has a security system at the front gate; residents have cards, and guests have to call and ask you to buzz them in. You can say no, but they can just follow someone and get in anyway. Your wife calls it pretend security.

You see the wide, distorted head of Claudia's mother through the peep hole. So this is it. This is the night that her daughter has gone missing. You don't remember her calling for the girl tonight. It's not a sound you would have missed. Whatever's happened, she's come to you for help. For some reason, this feels inevitable. You open the door.

The woman's face is red and puffy like she's been crying. Or she could be high. You're not expert enough to spot the difference. She's still wearing the candy stripe blouse and thin cotton shorts from earlier today. If she's been abused, it's impossible to tell. She has no visible bruises. The brothers are nowhere in sight.

"Can you help me?" she croaks. "My daughter is sick. She can't breathe."

"Claudia?" you ask. You want her to know that you

know her daughter's name. Why? To show her what a bad mother she is? To scare her? "Do you want me to call 911?"

"No, she has asthma. She just needs her medicine."

"I don't have any asthma medicine."

"I have a prescription," she says, "It's at the pharmacy, but our insurance . . . there's been a mix-up."

"Oh." This is sounding to you like one of those scams from a street person. My car broke down. I just need some gas. My son is handicapped. I need money for a cab. Living in Houston, you've heard a lot of these. Still, this woman is living right next to you.

"I just need twenty dollars and I can get her inhaler."

"Tonight?"

"The all-night pharmacy is holding it. I have a ride. I can get there. They said they'd hold it."

You pause. Asthma is serious business, and the woman could be telling the truth. "Just a minute," you say. You get your wallet from the bedroom, pull out a twenty. It leaves you with twenty-eight. At the door, you hand her the money. She leaves with a promise to pay you back. You know you'll never see the money again, but it was worth it for her to go away.

When Stacy gets home, she looks exhausted, tells you about another drunk ox that she had to keep in line. She could pass for a teenager, with her willowy arms and the casual cadence of her voice. She can take care of herself, that much is clear. But you still worry.

She asks about Charles's day. You tell her about the walk. "I'm not wearing that stupid carrier thing again. We'll have to find a different way to bond."

"I just wish I could see him more," she says. Sometimes, if the baby is up when she gets home, she'll take over the bottle or the diaper change. If he wakes in the night, she's usually too sleepy to handle it. "I don't even feel like his mother sometimes."

"Well, get a load of our mother next door," you say, and you tell Stacy about the money.

"When I was in the office to pay our rent," she says, "I heard they were behind on theirs."

"How did you hear this?"

"The manager isn't exactly professional."

"I wonder if someone called about that grill."

"Maybe they bounced a check."

"I hate to hear that," you say. "But not really." If they leave, your quality of life will certainly improve. But you also know that you might be fooling yourself. When they're gone, you might be forced to face your own problems.

"You did the right thing, baby," Stacy says, and pats you on the chest before she goes to bed.

The project you're working on is a video manual for a digital camera. You've built a following online by making fun of the genre of instructions. Most of it is conveyed in the tone of your voice. In truth, you stumbled onto the gimmick without even knowing what you were doing. You decided to walk through the very basics of an early generation iPhone, and almost immediately the comments said that you were hilarious. Now you have a Twitter account announcing new videos, where your fans respond with memes of cats with big eyes or blind musicians with the text "I See What You Did There."

Your channel inspires a series of inside jokes that you sometimes don't fully understand. What you post doesn't matter anymore; the draw is the comments section and the payoff is the social media imprint of each video. All you have to do is occasionally check in and comment, so it gives the illusion of being interactive.

You press record and hold up the camera you're reviewing. Hardly anyone buys digital cameras anymore, but most people who watch don't even own the product. You turn the camera upside down. "You can be sure the camera is oriented correctly if the red button marked PHOTO is facing up." You put your eye on the lens. "The large circle is the lens and should be pointed at the subject." You turn the lights out and try to take pictures in the dark. "The ideal conditions for taking crisp photos include a light source directed at the subject." You snap photos in the dark. "If your photos do not turn out well, you can check in the album and simply delete whatever doesn't suit your fancy." You never know which of your phrases will catch on, but usually something finds its way back in the comments.

Your son stirs in the other room, so it's time to turn the video off. You have about three minutes of useful material, which is short but still enough to post. When you reach the crib, Charles is not fully awake. You take a picture of him in the dark. The sound wakes him. From the other side of the apartment, you hear yelling through the wall. More F-bombs, but used in a different way. Someone has been cheating. How long has this fight been going on? You wonder if your video picked up any of the argument. Your son whimpers. You put the camera down.

When the child cries, it's your job to do something about it. When the neighbors start yelling, you should try as hard as you can to hear what the problem is. If it's about drugs, ignore it. If it's about cheating, you must try to hear every detail. Don't press your ear against the wall. Have some pride. Don't think about their child, how close her bedroom is, what she learns from the anger. You put your hand on your son's chest, and magically he falls back to sleep. The sounds from the neighbors fade into the night. *If it works, don't question it.*

You're fiddling with the digital camera the next day, scrolling through the pictures you took in the dark, when the husband knocks on your door. He doesn't have the baseball hat on, but he stands with the easy confidence of an athlete. His hair is fluffed just as the junior high boys used to do, shirt tucked like he's ready for a job interview. "I hear my wife borrowed some money from you." Before you have a chance to refuse, he's already gone to his wallet. No mention of what the money was for. You wonder if he even knows. Maybe he found out and cussed her for it. But his attitude here is calm, like this is a normal thing. *People do this. Borrow money, then pay it back.*

"Here you go," he says, and hands you a bill. You look in your hand. It's a ten. You look back and he's smiling like he's done you a favor. It's like he's expecting you to say thank you. "So there you go," he says, and he waits a little bit. You say, "All right," and he sees that he's gotten all he'll get out of you and walks away. You figure that this event has connected you now. You're both down ten bucks.

Every night Stacy's job wrings a little more out of her. You text her pictures of Charles when she's at work, but she doesn't respond. Lately when she comes home, even if the baby is up, she says she's tired and disappears into the bedroom.

You keep waiting for something to happen with the little girl next door. Each night, the mother still hollers for her to come home. *Clau-die! Clau-die!* You keep waiting to see which tragedy will be this family's undoing: Riding her bike into the traffic of the parking lot. Drowning. Disappearing.

You hate to admit that this is what you're watching for. Why does the world take care of some children and their reckless mothers, and others, with mothers who are good and trying their best to do the right thing, get left in the cold? You begin to think that there is a balance to the world, and the children who survive are in part responsible for the children who don't, and the mothers and fathers who are terrible take something away from the parents who try.

It's only the second time you've heard this knock, but you immediately recognize it as Claudia's mother. Insistent, formidable, but strangely soft. If a knock could be a question, that's what this is. You can't ignore it. Since they moved in, it feels like the doors and walls might as well be made of glass. As much as you sit in judgment of them, you feel their eyes on you, too.

Her hair frames her face in ringlets of dirty butter. She's been crying, it seems. Is this the end? Have they split up? Claudia is at her side, scowling.

"Could you watch Claudia for us?"

The exchange happens quickly, before you have time to think. Is it because she said "us" and not "me"? Is it because you feel guilty? When did this get so personal?

The door is closed and you haven't gotten a phone number. Only now does it occur to you that maybe today is eviction day. You peek through the blinds, but the mother has disappeared. Could they be leaving their belongings behind? The girl too?

"Your mother going somewhere?"

Claudia nods. "Your house is different."

You open the blinds and the sun streaks the coffee table. You're embarrassed about your mismatched furniture and you try to distract Claudia. "Our place is just like yours, except flipped," you say. "Like your apartment is looking in a mirror."

"Where's your baby?"

"Oh, you want to see the baby? He's right in here. I'll bring him out."

"What's his name?"

"Charles."

Claudia screws up her face. "How'd you think of *that*?"

You're not used to being challenged on the name, except by your own mother who disapproved so reliably of every suggestion that you stopped sharing them with her. "I don't know. I think it's a fine name," you say, but Claudia is not listening. She has grabbed your son's hand and opened it to look at his palm.

"His hand feels like rubber," she says.

"Careful. He's not a doll." You move to pick your child up and whisk him away from this girl, but he is smiling and gurgling. Claudia quickly bores of him and goes in search of something else to entertain her. Your son watches her walk away, and when she does not come back, his throat releases a whimper.

Claudia has found the television remote and mashes

buttons three at a time. "I think this is broken," she says. "Here," you say, "let me help you with that," but she has already let the remote slip to the floor and is off to the kitchen. "I'm hungry. I usually have mac and cheese for a snack."

By now, your son is whining, your final warning before he starts blasting the tears. You realize that you had expected Claudia to love your child, mother him like girls of her age are supposed to love to do. It didn't occur to you that your son might be the one to fall in love with her. You grab him in your arms before he lets loose. "Shh," you whisper in his ear. "You don't want a girl like that, no, no."

"I know how to make it myself," she calls. "I do it all the time."

"Oh really," you say, returning to the kitchen, holding Charles. "Your mother lets you do that?"

"She taught me how."

It's hard for you to get a picture of this. Does the woman scream in the child's ear? *Clau-die!! Don't add the milk until it's done! Clau-die! You got cheese dust on the stove!*

"Does your mother teach you a lot of stuff?"

Claudia shrugs, opens the pantry. "Where's the pan?"

"Actually, we don't have any mac and cheese." You say this with an air of superiority that surprises you. When you were a kid, you ate canned ravioli and twinkies and all the crap they convinced everyone that kids should eat. But now, that doesn't fly. You walk in the kitchen where your son can see Claudia again. He stills himself in your arms, stares as if he's spied a flamingo. *What is this creature?* You know it's not love he's feeling, but his tiny mind probably believes it is.

You need to call your wife.

You never call her unless it's an emergency. You want to appear competent. This one, though. This is as dangerous a situation as you can imagine.

Claudia opens more cabinets and you realize you will have to handle this yourself. "How about noodles? You can melt cheese on them." You expect her to object, but she shrugs and says okay. She takes the pan from you with confidence. "You sure you know how to do it?"

"I told you I do." She fills the pan with water to the right level and places it on the burner. She uses both hands, and the pan stays balanced. She turns the knob and coils begin to glow.

"Like a pro," you say, and mean it. You wonder if your child, completely helpless now, will transform in seven years into the capable child you see in front of you. For as maddening as Claudia is, she can take care of herself. That's your main job right now—caretaker—and this child doesn't seem to need you.

"What's that?" Claudia says. She's spotted the digital camera. You tell her and she says, "Let me see."

"Shouldn't you turn on the timer for the noodles?"

"I don't need to," she says, picking up the camera.

"It might be a good idea. If you forget, the water could boil over and the pan could burn. Maybe the whole kitchen."

"I won't forget," she says, putting the camera to her face.

"Here, let me show you how to use that."

"I know how to use it," she says.

You back off. Claudia studies the camera for a few moments, then presses the menu button. You smile because you know how much trouble you had with the settings. "There," she says, and turns the camera, surprisingly, to Charles. "Let's take pictures of the baby," she says, and pushes the button over and over.

Charles, as soon as Claudia turns her attention to him, tucks his chin to his chest and smiles. It's a coy smile, no teeth, his eyes waiting to see what kind of response this new person might offer him.

"Smi-le, ba-by," Claudia sings, and Charles responds by opening his mouth and pounding his fist like a delighted little dictator.

Hours pass. It's past dark. You helped Claudia with the boiling water for the noodles, but she did everything else herself. She's been playing with Charles and reading to him, patiently, but enough is enough. Stacy will be getting home soon. You've knocked on the door twice, no answer. The grill is gone from the porch, and you're afraid everything inside is, too.

Time to call Child Protective Services. But what will you say? You don't even know the woman's name. Surely the woman wouldn't have abandoned her daughter. Unless there was something more to be worried about. Before you can find the number, Claudia's mother returns.

"Claudie!" she says, and wraps her daughter in a hug. She does not ask you or her daughter if she behaved herself. She does not ask anything at all.

"It was no problem," you say, even though you haven't been thanked, and you mean it. A quick exchange of looks tells you what you already knew. Their apartment is empty. This is the last you'll be seeing of them. "Do you need," you say, "anything?"

She shakes her head, seems to be fighting back tears. "We have a place to go." You wonder how many backup plans this woman has had to maintain in her life.

Claudia runs outside, and you both watch her. A glossy Ford F-150 waits, running, in the lot. It's sprawled across two parking spots, at a careless angle. The windows are tinted, but you think you can see the shadow of the younger brother's bulky torso. The passenger door is propped open, and Claudia gets in.

Her mother touches your arm. "Thank you," she says. Her hand is soft and gentle, and even her voice touches you in the right way. "You've been a great neighbor," she says.

The mother gets in next to Claudia. The truck creeps backward, then stops. The passenger door opens, and Claudia hops out. For a moment you think she's coming back for a last look at the baby, but she has a set of keys in her hands. She runs and locks the front door to the apartment she's leaving behind. She stops and waves, at you, you think, before she climbs back in. You wave back.

When Stacy comes home, you're waiting up for her. You have something you have to tell her. Charles is asleep, exhausted after all the attention from Claudia. "I'm so glad you're home," you say.

She ignores you, probably thinks you're being ironic, like your YouTube persona.

"Our neighbors moved out today."

"So the manager was right?"

"I don't know, probably. I took care of Claudia."

"Who?"

"Claudia, their girl. Well, she took care of us, really.

Charles fell in love. A lot has happened." Your heart races. "You wouldn't believe."

Stacy throws her keys on the table. "I have to quit my job."

"I know. I mean, this girl, she makes her way. You start to think she can do anything."

"Babe, I'm telling you. I have to quit this job."

"Her mother, I still wouldn't do, couldn't do what she does. But what she withstands. I tell you, I have to reconsider what I thought of her."

"You're not listening."

"She is . . . I'll say it: She is an excellent mother."

"Babe."

"Yes I know." You look Stacy in the eye, exhilarated. "Of *course* you have to quit that job." You hold your wife close. You hold her like you're the one who's come home after a night of wandering, a night of crying, a night of trying to find your way. You are finally close enough to hear the voice that's been calling all this time. "It's so good," you say, "to hear your voice."

The Girl With One Arm

The boy was with the girl with one arm. They had been together long enough to know things about each other. He knew the name of the boy that had hurt her most, in third grade, and he knew that was the last time she'd let herself be hurt. He had revealed all the movies and books and bands that he loved, even the most embarrassing ones. But they had been together a short enough amount of time that afterwards, when he was alone, he had to rub his jaw from all the smiling he'd done. They had been together the perfect amount of time.

This was the night.

They sat on his sofa, the one covered with a thin blanket to hide the rips underneath, drinking root beer floats that he had made. He could not believe his luck. He looked at her face and it swam before his eyes and he was thinking how much he might love her, if he could only bring her into focus.

"So," the boy said, deciding he had waited long enough. "What's up with the one arm?" This boy was not one to mess around with too many words. It had taken him far too long, in his opinion, to come to this question. It was the question that popped into his head the very first time he saw her. This question meant everything.

He continued, "One of my friends thinks combine. Another thinks you must be some sort of fugitive."

"Birth affect." The girl always spoke very clearly, but sometimes the boy looked at her lips and his mind was somewhere else.

"You mean defect?"

"Nope."

The arm was gone up to the elbow. The boy was not shy of looking at it, or touching it for that matter, and neither was the girl shy of showing it. Her tops were almost always short-sleeved and often, like tonight, sleeveless.

The boy said, "Well, that's boring. I waited all this time for that? You sure there wasn't anything more?"

"That's it. All the genetic testing came back fine. No explanation." She sipped from the straw in her frosty mug. The boy liked to see her cheeks sink towards her open teeth. "My mom says my right arm is still in her, holding a death grip on her spinal cord."

The boy pictured a dark mother, foreign to him. He convinced himself that he could see the strength that had come through to her. He realized that he wanted the girl to speak to him in words he didn't understand. "You didn't want to come out?"

"Let's say I was conflicted." Her words slurred a bit, chilled by the ice cream drink. He wanted her tongue to shape the faint trace of an accent.

"Are you still conflicted?" The boy was not stupid. He realized that most questions that boys asked of girls were rephrasings of the question of all questions: *Do you like me?* and too, *How much do you like me?*

The girl, who was not stupid either, paused. The kind

of pause that helps one maintain balance, by keeping the other off-balance. This was one of her best skills. "That's the lovely part," she said, after enough pausing. "Part of me wanted to stay, part of me wanted to live here." She slurped the last of her drink loudly from the bottom of the mug. "And look who won."

"That was a fantastic root beer float," the boy said.

"You sure know how to make them," she said, as if sincere. This ability of hers to sound sincere when he knew she was being sarcastic was one of the things he loved about her. He felt this quality of hers was one of her purest elements, a square in her periodic table that had accompanied her from her beginning, and would stay with her until the last of her days.

He started to say something to her about elements and tables and atomic numbers, but he did not. He wanted to say impressive things to her, but he was afraid. Still, something of his disquiet must have come through to her because she said, "Maybe you shouldn't have used the caffeinated root beer."

The boy's heart raced. He spoke quickly.

"My friends say I'm only dating you because I think you're vulnerable. They tell me that I've never dated a girl who is as pretty as you, which is true. Without question." He pushed her hair back from her face and looked her in the eye. "They tell me I only had the nerve to talk to you because of the arm."

"Those friends of yours are something else. Are they real sweet talkers like yourself?"

"They call you Lefty."

The girl winced. "And you defend me. I can count on

this?"

"I would, but it's not you they're attacking."

"Then what do you say?"

"What can I say? The only other girl I've dated seriously had pneumonia when we met. It was walking pneumonia—nothing she had to be hospitalized for—but still I can't figure out how to prove them wrong."

"You could tell them _____," and the girl filled in the blank with an animated gesture, that of punching the friends in their imaginary faces. "I would show you the old one-two," she said, "but I don't think you're ready for that."

"Can you feel your arm?" the boy asked. He was becoming aware that this was the night that he wanted to learn about her body. That night always came with boys, especially young ones. The night they would try to lay bare those parts they could not see.

"Sure," she said, and she squeezed it with her hand.

"I'm being serious here."

"Oh really? Is that what's going on?"

"Yes, it is." He did his best to look injured, then he gave his report. "I just read something about what you can do with a mirror. If you're in pain, you can put a mirror up to one half of your body. You see your body whole, and it teaches your brain that nothing's wrong, and you shouldn't feel the pain." He believed that she had pain, pain that neither of them could see.

"Why would I want to do that?"

"I just thought you might want . . . " He waited for her to save him, but she would not. He would have to keep talking. "If it was hurting, that maybe you would want to stop it from hurting."

The girl was quiet for a minute and the boy believed she was processing how concerned he was, how caring. Then the girl looked at the boy's face and was instantly pleased. "You don't know what to call it."

Embarrassed, the boy quickly tried to change his tone. "My friends call it the stump."

She scrunched her nose.

"What?"

"I expect that from them. Not you."

"Okay, I admit it. I don't know what to call it. But it *is* important to me. As a matter of reference."

"What to call it?"

"I can't think of a good thing."

"How about *right arm*?"

The boy raised his finger. "I see where you're going there. You're going with literal. But that doesn't really capture it, does it? I mean, I can't think of a good *enough* thing. What about a word that cuts to the heart of things?"

"Why does it have to just be one word? Why must things be reduced?"

"I'm looking for essence. Plus, one word is efficient. It helps us understand."

The girl took a breath, as if she were going to respond at length. Then she turned away and said, "Nah."

"*Nah?* You give me *Nah?* Is that all you have?" His voice was rising, and he began to sweat. The muscles in his shoulders were tightening. He felt this was going very well.

"I thought you were in favor of one-word descriptions." She blinked at him slowly.

"I knew there was a reason I liked you."

He tried to pull her close to him, but she lightly pushed him away.

"The reason is this," she said, and she held it up. "The Arm Of Your Dreams."

He looked at her arm and he looked at the form it implied. "The arm of my dreams?"

"No," she said with contempt. "*The Arm Of Your Dreams.* It's a title, not a random pronoun. It's the same no matter who is speaking of it."

"So if anyone asks, I'm supposed to say, 'I fell in love with her because I saw *The Arm Of Your Dreams*?'"

The boy looked at the girl and he could tell that she heard what he said, that it really registered with her, the part about "fell in love," because her voice softened a bit as she said, "That's right. Because it's whatever a person dreams it to be."

The boy could not have foreseen any of this, but it had been a surprisingly easy thing to say. He felt a part of himself let go, and he listened to himself say other easily said things.

"Whatever I dream?" The boy moved closer. "Long, creamy, lovely?"

"Mmm."

"Bewitching?" He bent his head to her shoulder.

"Mmm."

"Tender, warm?" He closed his eyes.

"Shriveled," she said, loudly. "Knobby. Cancerous."

He stiffened a bit. "I see."

"Bloody. Burned."

He sat up. "Yes, I get it."

"Leprous . . ."

"Enough!" He raised his hands in the air, his body

tense. He would not look at her.

"Come here," she said, but he could not tell if she was sincere. "Let me rub your back. Let me rub it with The Arm of Your Dreams."

He felt her hand tug on his shirt, but he pulled away. "How do I know it's not a hook?"

"Only you can know your dreams," she said. "Take off your shirt."

He complied. This was not how he'd imagined things going, but he complied.

"Now lay down. That's it. No," she said, without touching him. "No looking back. Close your eyes."

He waited. This moment felt close to what he had wanted, but he was not sure. He sensed movement above him.

The girl asked, "Do you feel anything?"

"No," said the boy, and he felt her disappointment cool the air.

"You need to relax," she said. "There. How about now?"

"Yes," he lied, because he thought it was still possible to lie to her. "I can feel something. Can you?"

"Not yet," she said, "But I'm trying. Are your eyes closed? You have to promise to keep your eyes closed."

The words came to him very easily. "I promise." He could say them again if she asked, he was sure. He loved her for trying to touch him with her missing hand, no matter what happened. The evening was darkening, and he could feel the air from an open window across his body. He was about to tell her this was all he wanted. He was about to tell her how much he loved her in this moment when he felt a finger of warmth on his right shoulder. A knot of breath issued from his lips.

"There."

One, two more fingers. A hand. Rubbing. The invisible hairs on his skin tingled. He did not have to tell her he felt it. It was clear and distinct, unmistakable. Then it was gone. So quickly that he wasn't sure it had happened. He waited, but the feeling did not return.

"I want to see it," he said. "Please, I want to see it."

"Oh baby, you know better."

He relaxed his body back into the sofa, and there it was again. A hand, touching him on his skin, reaching deep beneath the surface. Eyes still closed, in his mind he saw her hand at the end of The Arm Of Your Dreams, and it looked the same as her other hand, a mirror image of it, with no defect, every knuckle, every bone in it whole. It occurred to him, of course it did, that she could just be rubbing his back with her left hand.

"I can touch you like this, with The Arm Of Your Dreams, as often as you like."

This is what it must feel like to be a god, he thought. Nothing to him before had felt so good. His skin hummed. Oh, things were moving fast, as things can. He was the happiest boy on earth. That is, he should have been. Inside, some other thing worked on him. He felt another hand on his throat, squeezing. It made him tense. It made him say other things.

"Is this something we'll always have, you and I?"

"Yes," she said, her voice assuring. "As long as you keep your eyes closed."

Her hand moved to more sensitive areas of his body. He felt as if he were being kissed thoroughly, inside and out. A thought occurred to him and his body tensed. "Have you felt this before?"

"Never." This time, there was no pause.

Immediately, he relaxed again. *Never.* One word. The essence of the thing. But that other hand inside him squeezed his throat so hard he gave a little jerk and without knowing what he was doing, he almost opened his eyes.

"Oh baby, don't. Don't you want everything? Don't you want what you can see and what you can't? Don't give away what you can't see. Let's not give it away."

"I didn't know," he said. What was it they had?

"All of it is ours."

He felt her hand on his ear, or was it inside? It was like listening to the sea. It was almost too much for him. I'll drown, he thought, and even though he didn't speak she seemed to hear him anyway.

"Shh. Don't look. I'll turn to salt. Just like they say. Don't look."

He felt a shiver rise in his back. "Just let me turn over. I want to feel you everywhere."

"You can't. It will be too difficult for you." She waited, and he thought she was relenting, but she said again, firmly, "No."

He felt an ending coming, a relief, but then the hand on his throat squeezed out these words. "How do I know you're not lying?" It was only as he said this that he understood the challenge. He whispered, "Put your other hand on me."

Silence. The hand, whichever hand was on his back, seemed to throb.

"Maybe we should just watch a movie. Weren't we going to watch movies tonight?"

"Do this for me," he said. "Prove it to me."

"To you? You, who have proven nothing to me?"

He wouldn't let her provoke him. He knew he was winning. "Give me a chance. Just give me the chance and I will."

He could feel his sincerity beginning to crack the distance above him.

"But that one is cold. It's the hand I used to hold the drink."

"I don't care."

"Lay down," she said. "Keep your eyes closed."

"I'll keep them closed. I won't look."

"I can't promise anything."

"I understand."

He felt the hand of The Arm Of Your Dreams once again. His muscles melted beneath the touch and he forgot what else it was he wanted. Wasn't there something else? How could there be? And then a circle hit him on his left side, cold and damp, that nearly shocked his eyes open, but he held true. A circle?

"The mug!" He giggled. His world, which had been in a shuffle, suddenly sorted itself out.

"No, it's not," she said.

She sounded serious, but she couldn't be.

"You put the mug on my back," he said, but immediately doubted it. He twisted a bit, but the cold pressure remained. "You're a witch!" he teased, but anything was possible.

"I'm doing what you asked," she said. "I'm giving you everything."

The circle began to warm into the shape of a palm, and above it, five fingers pressing into his flesh. Two arms. Two hands. "I have to turn over," he said. "I feel like my body will fly apart. You have to let me turn over."

"No. That's not how this works."

He expected her hands to push on his back and keep him down. But the pressure stayed the same, maybe even lightened.

"I'll keep my eyes closed," he said desperately. He thought he felt his back rise, to meet the full pressure of her hands again.

"You say that, but what if you open them? Even an accident will be too much."

"But . . . I want all of you."

"You have all of me. You have it now."

She kept rubbing his back. He still felt both hands on him, and it still felt wonderful, and he did not want her to stop, but a little of the surprise was gone. He could feel it leaking away.

"You have to make your choice now, with your eyes closed," she said. "Is this what you want of me? What you have now, is this what you want? Is this enough for you?"

"Yes, yes, it's enough," the boy said, not knowing what he meant.

"But I have to turn over now." He knew if he opened his eyes, she would be gone to him forever. He began to weep. "Come closer," he said, turning his body.

"Do not do this," she said, but still she came closer.

"Even closer," he said. He was being very deliberate. He felt a tear drop from her eye onto his cheek. He felt two hands grab him, he knew there were two of them, one on each arm. He lost track of which touch was The Arm Of Your Dreams and which the arm he'd always known, and soon he lost track of his own body.

"I know how you think this is going to end," he told her. "The boy will open his eyes, and the girl will disappear. Isn't that right?"

"Forever," she said.

"Come closer," he said, and he felt her lips next to his. "My eyes are closed," he said, and this time he hoped she could see he was not lying. Her lips came to his in a kiss, and he felt them wet and warm, and her hands loosened their grip on him, and he could not describe any of it in a single word or even more because he had lost track of his questions but it was still like nothing else and he was trying to keep up and night must have fallen and he could barely locate his own body in space because he could not see, in spite of himself, anything.

The Marks

It didn't take long to understand that the marks that had appeared on everyone's skin weren't going away. At first they looked like birthmarks, light-brown ponds. Some thought this a sign of age until we noticed them on the children. We blamed the sun and rubbed lotion on the skin of the affected and the unaffected. The spots were not painful or warm or raised or textured. They seemed benign, but they did not fade. Soon they became darker brown then went to black, distinct on every skin tone, narrowing into defined lines, squiggles, and shapes. No amount of washing or abrasion would take them away. It was as if they emerged from deep inside, marks awaiting maturity before they appeared. Then we observed something striking.

A group of us noticed that these marks, if put together, could form a letter, a word, possibly more.

The first letter anybody remembers was a *C*. It was formed by the left arm of a young girl touching the right cheekbone of her brother. Both parents denied that it was a letter, in part because they didn't want people coming into their house, but also because of a suspicion of what their own eyes had seen. Word soon spread in spite of their objections, and entire neighborhoods went to see the letter: an arc of perfection when placed at the proper angle.

The next letter, an *H*, took a few weeks to appear, made by juxtaposing the calf of our fire chief with the pinkie finger of the oldest woman in town. Some accused them of copycatting, writing on their skin in marker for the attention it would bring, but those who saw in person knew the sheen of the marks in the light—the matte finish of a coffee bean—and all soon admitted it was authentic.

Someone is *speaking* to us, from without, some thought. Others: No, these are *messages* emerging from within. Or: No, this is just who *we* are. There is nothing to it.

After that, the letters came in a cavalcade. It was impossible to keep track of which letters had appeared first. Neighborhoods appointed official recorders to transcribe the most local messages. There were arguments. Some panicked. They thought that any misstep meant that the message intended for us would be garbled. Others thought that the messages were meant to come in fragments, that we should bring them to the town proper and stitch each unit together like a quilt.

The combinations were endless. Wherever people gathered, they formed words. One person's marks could be used in several passages of the message. A belief overtook us that there was only one message, slowly revealing itself. For us to understand the message, all had to reveal the marks to each other. Those who wouldn't reveal their marks were either forced to gather or they were shunned. Some left our village altogether. It wasn't until later that we realized the loss.

Part of the message was gone.

Suddenly these people were considered more valuable than those who had stayed. We sent some to search for them, to try and bring them back into our community. But those we sent didn't return, and we didn't risk losing any others.

It was decided that a group should be formed to determine which parts of the message to write down as scripture, but immediately we discovered that half a dozen groups had already begun this process, unbidden. One group would interpret a fragment as complete, but another thought it was yet unfinished. Nobody knew whether the messages were isolated and intended for just a few, or connected and intended for the body of us. Some of us tried to remain true to the exact letters and words, in the precise order they were revealed. But others rearranged the letters into words that were already familiar to us, and the words into sentences that made sense to us. It's only logical, they said, that the messages would come to us in a language that we would understand. These were the people who believed the messages were meant to be laws. No, said others, we are meant to learn something new about language. These were the people who believed the messages were poetry. Still others, those who believed the messages were prophecy, asked: If we are being told things we already know, then what is the point?

Sometimes the messages were funny. Silly jokes. We wondered if we were being mocked. Others thought it was a gift, the humor a respite from our suffering. For a time all of the messages lost their meaning for us, became absurd, hilarious.

Some of us began to drift from the marks altogether, obeying other impulses. The shyest woman, Analinda, began wearing tall, frilly hats because she believed she was being directed to do so. Another woman, Hoa, when she went for her daily walk, turned her torso at an angle toward the trees, blessing them as she went. She grew resentful because she believed a man named Fredric was supposed to walk parallel to her, blessing the trees on the other side. She left a pile of stones in front of his door as tribute to his neglect. One group of men shaved every hair on their bodies to wholly reveal the marks. Another group of men threw their razors away, believing the marks should be read through obscurity. Some followed baser impulses, using the promise of the marks as an excuse to engage in the pleasures of the body.

No approach could be agreed upon. There were enough factions to sustain many groups, meeting separately. And the messages were so easy to interpret differently, we were comfortable with this new separation.

Then the marks began to change.

A line on a cheek slipped down the face like a teardrop. Some angles developed crooks like shepherds' staffs; the jagged turned smooth. Some feared we had been using the wrong alphabet, that maybe we were being given a language that none of us could—or should—understand. We feared that these messages might not be meant for us at all, but for a faraway audience of the lost.

First the changes came monthly, then weekly, hourly. The marks would be clear, then melt, fade, and darken in a moment into a completely different character. In the middle of readings the marks would change, so we would scramble to rearrange ourselves, tracking the new meaning.

Some brought permanent markers to the meetings, to trace the lines of the original marks so they wouldn't be lost. These originalists called themselves the Everlasters. Others called the Everlasters heretics, holding on to the messages of the past, ignoring the messages of the current time. But the marks changed so much that even the Everlasters could no longer determine what message was original.

It was during one of the Everlaster sessions that a child named Lily noticed the trees had a kind of mark, too. Those are different marks, some said, but others insisted they could be read as a message, too. Then we looked to the grass and animals and even that which was inanimate like steel or light—some saw marks in all of them.

Everything was marked.

We realized what we should have known all along: any moment was a gathering. It didn't matter who was or wasn't there to receive or interpret. Messages piled up like leaves. They couldn't be recorded fast enough. Any time was a gathering, any time holy.

This marked our greatest crisis.

Some groups wouldn't gather with other groups. Some people refused to read altogether. Others kept themselves hidden. If every gathering was holy, every moment transcendent, then some thought that *all* moments were the same and therefore not holy.

We stopped transcribing the messages. Soon, we stopped translating them altogether. We had been spoken to enough.

We passed the stories to our children. We taught them all we knew. Our children have always known our marks, so when they look upon them, they see nothing wondrous. Now when they see the marks on their bodies, these marks that assuredly still appear, they consider them, if they consider them at all, as ornament. They do not listen to us in the same way. The oldest of us believe that the marks have faded, that they were stronger in the older days. Some no longer see them at all, even those with the best eyesight. Some suggested long ago that one will come who will read the message to us.

People do not gather anymore. A few of us wait for the interpreter, alone, but most have given up hope. Most believe the answer has already arrived.

Moths

Collecting moths was Frank's idea. It didn't make any sense to me because it wouldn't help the soldiers, and you couldn't get any money for doing it, either. We were collecting all sorts of other things for the war effort at the time. I walked the neighborhoods piling my wagon with old copies of the *Grand Rapids Press* on Sunday evenings, and the rest of the week I'd collect tin cans and any other scrap metal I could find. One time I found a whole front bumper off of a '37 Dodge. The scrap man I sold it to whistled and said, "Jerry, they're probably gonna make a battleship outta this." Even though I wanted to, I don't think I believed the man. Still, collecting scrap metal seemed much more practical than collecting moths, but Frank didn't care. He didn't wait for someone else to tell him something made sense before he went ahead and did it.

This was summer 1943, in the middle of a war that nobody could see the way to the end. All the dads like mine who hadn't been drafted felt bad about it. We heard stories of granddads who tried to enlist but got sent back by the recruiting officers, saying they would do more good with their families. My dad tried to sign up, but they told him he was too old. He seemed happy enough doing his part at the factory, making chairs and listening to Tigers games on the radio instead of the war news.

Mother was different. She listened to every report with her head bent to the speaker, like if she worried enough it would help bring an end to the fighting. She had fastened black shades to the windows for the nighttime air raid drills, and she followed the directions to the letter. She kept up our ration books for sugar and gasoline. The whole country was tightening: there weren't even any new cars being made. The only time I saw Mother happy was when she told stories about the play parties she used to go to where the teenagers would dance and sing and eat whatever candies and cakes they wanted. Before the war, she used to sing me some of the songs. After these years of war, she told the stories with a look in her eye like she was remembering those times, but she never sang. I think she was in just as much of a fight as anyone, fighting an idea of what she must have thought her life should have been like: nice dinner parties, dancing, a cottage on the lake for summers. I wished I could save up money and get her something nice, something that would make her sing again. Mother never talked about these times when Dad was around, and I always wondered why.

We lived on very little. I don't remember having a new pair of jeans. I wore my brother John's, then Dad's. When I was done, my stuff went to little Robby, only by then it was so worn that sometimes he'd get new stuff. I only wore shoes five months out of the year. Mother told me the soles were rationed like everything else. So I said, "Frank Petterson got some and he didn't have a ration book." And she said well his momma used her own rations for him and that's when I told her that Frank's momma was dead.

None of the other kids liked Frank. He was a strange guy. He stood like his skull was fused to his spine so that he couldn't turn side to side. "Looks to me like that boy's been in an accident," my dad said, and maybe he had but I never asked him. People at school called him names. Gerald Stuckey had caught Frank hanging around the cemetery, and he never let him forget. "Hey Gravedigger, you use a shovel or your hands? Lemme see. Yep, got dirt under those nails all right." They said he dug up the corpses from their graves and kept their body parts behind his house. I never wanted to believe them, but then I wasn't in any hurry to dig around Frank's backyard.

One time Frank was over and all of us boys were in the garage when my dad was changing the oil on the Ford. Frank made my dad nervous. Frank's skin was paper white with dark spots around his eyes. Plus, he had a birthmark the color of raw beef that covered most of his cheek and half his lips. The first time I ever saw him I thought he must have been in a big fight. I thought he looked like a pretty tough guy; after all, at fourteen he was two years older and quite a bit bigger than I was. But I was wrong. He got beat up a lot. Gerald and his crowd jumped him so often that he seemed used to it. I asked him one day why he didn't fight back. "You're bigger than anybody in the school," I said.

He shrugged. "After a couple of punches, I don't even feel it." He said it with pride. For that, I was a little envious of Frank.

Dad crouched down and put the oil pan underneath the plug. My brothers and I already knew how to change the oil, but this demonstration was for the benefit of

Frank, so I showed interest like I was supposed to. Frank stood like a coat rack, breathing through his mouth. "See here?" Dad said. "Here's the pan." I nodded, but then Dad looked at Frank, who was looking at the front hubcap. "Next we loosen the plug. Come on over here where you can see, young man." Frank bent down and peered at the undercarriage, but he didn't seem to be looking in the right direction. "Can you point to the plug, Frank?" Frank pointed to the battery. John and Robby giggled at Frank. "No," Dad said, and he tapped the plug with a wrench. "Over here. You see that?" Frank nodded, and Dad looked at me, shrugged, and went on with the lesson. Later he told me, "A boy that age ought to know more than he does. But Jerry, it's not his fault. It's the father's fault." Then Dad thought better of that and said, "But you can't blame him either, I suppose." I knew what all that meant: he blamed both Frank and his father.

I had only seen Frank's father once, when he came to pick up Frank early from school the day his momma died. He was big as a bear so that's what they called him. His hair was greasy and he filled up the cab so that I remember wondering how Frank would fit in there, too. Bear Petterson was unemployed, a strange thing in those times. He hadn't been seen in town lately, and some weren't even sure he was still around. "Seems to me a man doesn't have a job, he doesn't *want* to work," Dad said. He didn't name names, but it was clear who he was talking about. And it was clear that he was warning me about Frank.

Frank's dad might have been scary, and Frank might not have known things like how to change the oil in a car, but I felt like Frank knew things that the other kids did not. Things that your parents and your teachers didn't tell you. For one, he was the only person I knew who didn't care about collecting things for the war effort. Two, he got beat up and seemed to enjoy it. Three, he didn't care that the other kids teased him. And also he was big and a little scary looking. So I suppose calling him my friend was my way of being a little brave, too.

I think I also felt sorry for Frank because, in spite of the abuse he took sometimes, people forgot about him. Just like I was forgotten sometimes. John was the oldest so he got all the responsibility, and Robby was the youngest and had the most need. I won't lie, though— sometimes not being noticed was an advantage.

The only reason I ever went to Frank's house in the first place was because I thought he had something really valuable there. "It's like nothing you've ever seen," he'd said. I thought maybe it was something we could sell, so I could maybe get something nice for Mother.

Frank lived a few blocks away in a part of town that wasn't quite a neighborhood and wasn't quite country, either. The place was hidden by oaks and birch trees with peeling bark about as ramshackle as the house itself. They had a big front yard and a wide porch. I could hear chickens clucking in the distance. "Come on out back," Frank said, kind of slurping as he talked. "I want to show you something."

This is when I really started to consider what Gerald and the other boys said about graves and body parts. His stride was so long, it was hard to keep up with him. I saw something move on the ground and jerked my head. A pile of leaves began to rise and so did the hair on my head. I want to say it was the wind and not a body rising from the ground, but I can't say for sure because I ran to catch up with Frank.

Just as we turned the corner of the porch, there was a rattle at the front door. I didn't want to run back toward the rising leaves, but I also didn't want to see what was about to come out of the house. I held my breath. The door creaked open, and I saw the greasy hair hanging off the head of Frank's father. He wasn't wearing a shirt and his chest sort looked sort of soft like a woman's. The sun couldn't have been behind him but it still felt like he cast a shadow over both of us. This bear of a man walked out on the porch, and Frank froze.

Bear scratched his belly and took in a deep breath. He gazed out over his property. He did not look our way. "Boy? Who you brought there?" There was a lot of white to his eyes and I'm not sure they ever moved. I wondered if he might be blind.

"This is Jerry." Frank's voice trembled a bit. "I'll just take him out back."

The man smelled the air like he was trying to understand something. Then he nodded a little sadly, and turned and went back in the house. He got smaller as he moved away from us and disappeared into the darkness.

I wondered if Frank had ever brought anyone else over to house. I doubted it. I was probably the first. All I knew was, I never wanted to see that Bear Petterson again.

"Come on," Frank said. His voice was steady again, like he'd already forgotten all about his father's presence.

We walked through a flurry of chickens beating their wings in the dirt. "Back here," Frank said. He opened the door to a tiny shed with two big screens on the back wall that let in the light. After all the ruckus with the chickens I was expecting more animals or something inside, but the shed seemed still and quiet.

"You have to promise to stay still so you won't hurt them. No matter what happens, don't move."

This was just the kind of strange situation my parents had warned me about. I knew what I was supposed to do. I was supposed to turn and run away. I was supposed to have done that when I saw old Bear Petterson scratching his naked belly. But I was here. I'd come this far.

"Okay," I said.

Frank opened a box with what looked like a net inside, and I could hear the fluttering of wings. Not like the chickens. It was a whisper on the back of my neck. Then I saw the shadow of one against the light of the screen. It looked like a small bird. I thought maybe they were doves, or pigeons, but they'd have to be the quietest birds I'd ever heard of. Suddenly the shed was alive with the flying. I caught sight of the wings on one. It looked like the markings on the wings of the Zeros airplanes. Just as one flew at my face I started to cringe, but Frank said, "Don't," so I relaxed. It landed on the top of my head, I was sure, though I couldn't feel anything.

"What are they?" I asked.

"Moths," Frank said. "I figured out how to keep them in here." He balanced one on his index finger and brought it to my eyes. By now I'd adjusted to the dim light, and I could see that it did not look like a plane at all but had the most vivid markings I'd ever seen on a moth. It looked like the edge of a lake that left a crimson ring on shore. I knew that this was a test of sorts, and even though I knew I wasn't supposed to use the word because it was kind of sissy I said, "They're beautiful." Frank didn't have any reaction. He just kept looking at the moth on his finger and the wings flexing in the frail light.

It wasn't long before I had a clutch of cocoons on a side screen of my front porch. I hadn't fully given up on the idea that I could sell them, that they must be worth something to somebody. They were attached to little twigs I'd hung on the screen, and they were wrapped in something that looked like a really tight spider web. Bits of leaves and tiny insects would catch on the loose strands. My folks weren't crazy about the idea, but they didn't try to stop me, either. Dad would ask me most every day, "How are the bugs coming along?"

Mother said, "Just make sure those caterpillars don't get into my garden. If they do, that will be food out of your mouth, not mine."

She was talking about her victory garden. It was not ours. It was hers. She shared the food with us. We were all doing our part, with every bite we ate. And we were all on a strict ration. If she boiled squash, she counted the slices. She never talked about it, but I could look over at my brothers' plates and count, eight slices apiece. Mother and Dad, both eleven slices. Nobody asked for seconds, not even Dad. We knew everything had been portioned correctly, and at the next meal it would be so again.

When school let out for summer, Frank came over every day to help check on the cocoons. Once when we went in the house, Mother asked Frank about the moths. "Does your father know you're doing this?" Frank said, "I don't think he cares, ma'am." Mother nodded her head like that was the answer she expected. She suggested we do something better with our time, and from then on I made sure to keep Frank out of the house and on the porch.

Frank didn't like to talk, so I asked a lot of questions. When I ran out of new questions, I asked the old ones again.

"You sure we don't have to feed them?"

He shook his head. "They don't need to eat. They're done eating."

"Forever?" I asked.

"For as long as they live," he said. "They won't even have a mouth."

"Why not?"

"Won't need it. Everything they needed to eat has already been stored up."

"How long will they live?" I asked, knowing it wouldn't be long.

He shrugged. "A couple of weeks. Maybe not that long."

By this time I knew they weren't worth any money, but I was still anxious to see them. "Are you sure they won't come out now?"

"Nope. We have to wait until spring."

I kept the cocoons on the porch all through the fall. I even sort of forgot about them once the cold set in. But every now and then I checked on them. At school one day in November I told Frank about it.

"There's snow all over them. I tried to brush it away, but then they just ice over."

"Don't worry about it. They'll be all right. If they weren't on your porch, they'd be outside on a lilac bush somewhere."

I suppose it made sense when he put it like that, but I

just didn't see how those moths that I had seen last summer could survive anything as harsh as a Michigan winter. Those cocoons must have been some feat of engineering.

That winter someone all the way from the war office came to take pictures of Dad at the American Seating factory. Since the war they had been manufacturing barracks chairs. I was hoping Dad might bring one home for us, but he said "our boys" needed all of them and didn't have any to spare. Dad was pretty excited about the pictures, and I was too. I even said something about it in front of the whole class at school, and I had never done anything like that before.

The teacher, Mrs. Linney, had me stand in front and say what the plant did before the war. I didn't exactly know, so I talked for a bit and then made up a few things. I said, "They even made some chairs that the President may have sat on." I peeked over at her when I said it and she didn't give me a mean look or anything, so I figured maybe it was true. "And now the Secretary of War himself is coming to take a picture of my dad."

When I said that I accidentally looked at Frank, and then he looked down like he didn't see me. I figured he must be embarrassed that his own dad didn't have a job. I didn't mean to make him look bad, but thought I probably had.

I didn't get to see the Secretary of War, and it turned out that Dad didn't, either. Something came up and he sent one of his staff members. But it was still a big show with a senator and even the governor, and that very night we all got to see the picture in the paper.

Mother clipped it right out and pinned it to a cork board in the kitchen with two ends of a broken sewing needle. Everybody in the picture looked like they were having a grand time. It was taken on the factory floor and you could see the windows and steam pipes in the background. Dad was putting a clamp on the underside of one of the chairs, even though he told us he never worked on the line anymore. The picture stayed on the board for about a week, then one day I noticed it was gone. I didn't say anything, but Dad finally asked about it.

"Geneva, where's the picture?"

She tilted her head as if to say, *what picture?*

"The one from the paper. With the governor. Our district manager is coming in, and I'd like to show it to him."

"Oh." She didn't look Dad in the eye. "The boys came by with the wagon." She wiped the kitchen table with a dishrag.

I think Dad already knew what had happened. He said, "The wagon."

"Mm. The boys came to collect, and I put it in with the rest of the papers." She said this with a ring of fact that made it impossible to respond to. He stood there for a while, but I'm not sure he was even looking at her.

Later that afternoon Dad sat in the den. Baseball season was over. The Tigers had finished 78-76. "Just good enough to keep you coming back," Dad said. This time he was listening to a football game. Michigan State was his favorite, but they didn't even field a team this year. Their coach went off to help with the Camp Grant Army team. I asked him who was playing, but I'm not sure he heard me.

I put on my slippers and muffler and went out on the porch to check the cocoons. I knew what I would find, but I checked them anyway. Cold and hard. I counted them every time, and there were still twelve. I touched them because Frank told me I wouldn't hurt them if I did it carefully. I touched each of them once, with the tip of my finger, and I wondered if maybe they could feel just a little bit of warmth.

Sometime in February, I started losing touch with Frank. He stopped coming to the house, which I didn't think much of because it was a pretty bad winter. He missed a lot of school, too. He would always be back after a few days, wearing clothes a little dirtier, a little more ragged. Then pretty soon he stopped coming to school altogether. Mrs. Linney finally asked about him in class. Some of the kids said his dad made him get a job. One kid said he saw him at the butcher's, but Frank had acted like he didn't know him. Gerald said, "Check the graveyard. That's where all the spooks are."

I was worried. A little about Frank, but more about me. It was late April and the weather had started turning warm. I knew the cocoons were about to hatch, and I didn't know what to do. Wherever he was, I had to find Frank.

That evening, Mother and Dad had a dinner invitation from the VanStratens down the street. As soon as they left, I would go to Frank's house.

As Mother was getting ready, Dad came in and handed her a pretty velvet hat. It was the kind of gift I wanted to get her, to remind her of those times she liked best. She reached for it and looked up at him. She had the look in her eye like she did when she was about to sing. Then she put the hat on the dressing table.

"It's too much," Mother said. "I can't wear something like that. Not now."

"What does it matter?" Dad said. "You already *have* it."

Mother continued to brush her hair. "We shouldn't even go."

Dad picked up the hat and, because it looked like he didn't know what else to do with it, twirled it on his hand.

Mother put the brush down. "But we will, because I told them we would." She looked at me. "And you will do what your brother John says. Be in bed when we get back. Not a minute after nine."

When they left, it was dusk. John agreed to watch after Robby and told me not to get lost because then it would be his fault. I'd have to return the favor to him someday, and I would. I put on my boots and hat and walked toward Frank's house. If he wasn't there, I wasn't sure where else to look.

There was just a sliver of a moon. When I got outside of town I could hear the owls in the distance. I thought about turning back, but knew I couldn't. This was something I had to do.

I was afraid Frank's house would be hard to find in the dark, but I saw a light on through the window. I walked up to the front porch. I did not want to see Bear Petterson again, but if that's what it took to find Frank, I would do it. I knocked on the door.

Frank opened it. He looked the same to me, maybe a little taller.

"Is your dad home?"

Frank shook his head. "He's gone." The way he said it, I knew Bear was really gone. Frank was alone.

Cereal bowls lined the coffee table, fragments of Corn Flakes crusted to them. Books and newspapers were strewn on the floor. The couch had a blanket and a pillow on it, and Frank's clothes looked and smelled like he'd been sleeping in them for weeks. "Frank," I said. "What are you going to do?"

"I'm all right."

"You haven't been at school."

He just looked at me.

"The cocoons. They're going to hatch," I said. "I need your help."

"No you don't. You'll figure it out."

I had to wonder if that's what Bear Petterson told his son when he left. I tried to talk Frank into coming back to school. I even suggested he come live with us. "My folks would let you," I said, but he probably heard in my voice that I wasn't sure. In fact I was not sure that Mother would divide what little we had yet another way.

"Thanks," he said, and he looked around the house like he was trying to find something. "I have some things to take care of. It might take me some time."

"That's okay," I said. "Come whenever you can."

"Okay, I will," he said, and I hoped he would. He gave me a flashlight so I could find my way back home, and I told him I'd return it when he came to the house.

That was the last I saw of Frank. Some people said he lied about his age and joined the service. I checked his house just to make sure, but all I found were a couple of raccoons and broken dishes. Back in the shed where he'd kept his moths, there were a few sticks and a couple of broken and empty cocoons.

As spring began to warm, I kept hoping Frank would show up, but of course he didn't. The middle of May, two of the moths emerged. In another six days, all twelve were out. Frank had tried to tell me the difference between males and females, but I wasn't very good at seeing it. All I knew was, they were beautiful. My whole family stopped using the front door so we could keep them in the porch. The moths flew around at night in front of the light and put on a real show. Dad pretended to complain sometimes, but I think he liked them. Even Mother seemed to enjoy them. They were really something to look at. And I felt like I'd done it, I'd made it happen, something strange and wonderful, something like Frank might have done. Something that not many people could even understand. I could even get them to land on my finger and fan their wings. It was all they had left to do, really. Flap those wings.

That, and make more just like themselves. Even though I didn't know which was which, I thought I had a mix of males and females. I hoped they could figure things out because I wasn't sure how to help them along, and the only thing I wanted was to make sure they would keep going because it didn't seem right for them to just come to an end.

On the fourth night I had them out, a police car drove up with its lights on. I figured maybe it had something to do with an air raid drill, but I hadn't heard any sirens. One of the officers shone a flashlight into the porch and I had to shield my eyes. "Please don't open the door," I said. "They'll get away."

"What do you have there, young man?" He put the

beam in each corner of the porch.

"Moths. They're called Cecropia."

"They're quite a sight," the other one said. They both just stood there for a minute, taking in the flight of the moths. "They're big as bats."

I didn't know what to say. "They don't bite."

They both kind of laughed. "I know son," the one with the flashlight said. "But we got a complaint from someone on the block. You got somebody scared about what's going on over here."

"Somebody's scared of moths?" I said.

"Are your folks home?" the other one said.

I got Dad to come out on the porch. He looked a little embarrassed that the police were at our door. They talked for a while about air raid drills, and something about the light being on at night, and other things that didn't make any sense to me, and then they said something about letting them go.

"But Dad," I said, and I could tell by his face that he'd already decided. He was going to do what the policemen wanted. Before Dad could do it I went to the door and held it open. Dad turned out the light. It took a long time, longer than I thought it would, for them to get the last moth outside. I watched them go because I felt like I owed them that, and I thought about Frank, all those blows that he took.

After the war, things were much happier in our house, just like they were in most everyone's. We had plenty of food to eat, and my brother and I got new clothes whenever we needed. Eventually we got a television, and a second car. Mother and Dad went out every weekend and although she didn't wear that velvet hat, she did buy several others and wore them everywhere. She didn't get her summer cottage, but we did move into a bigger house. She kissed Dad every night, on the lips, when he came home from work.

Not too long ago, I was thinking about the moths again and mentioned them to Mother and how silly it was for the police to come to our house because of a bunch of harmless moths. "I bet it was that old lady across the street," I said. "What was her name?"

"Mrs. Richter," she said.

"That's right. That old crank. Doing something like that to a little kid."

Mother turned. "You cannot blame that woman for calling the police," she said. "She was only doing what she knew to do. You do *not* understand the times we were living in, and I'm not sure you ever will."

I saw a lean look in my mother's eye, a look I hadn't seen since those years long ago. I remembered the suspicious way she looked at Frank when he came over to the house. And then I knew. It was her. She had called the police. On me, on her own son.

I never accused her. I never had to. And I decided not to blame her, either. She was right. Those were different times. Then was a time of rationing. Everything collected, everything we did without, made a difference. After the collecting, it was time to set free.

Triumph, Only Triumph

Snow was coming down hard, better than an inch an hour according to the radio. Ed Wilson's wife Winnie had gone to dinner with friends from the non-profit where she volunteered, unaware that the worst blizzard of the decade was blowing in. Maybe that was overstating it, but they liked to overstate things on the radio, and in fact, Ed didn't mind the exaggeration. It gave him a mission. He had to get that drive shoveled for her. She was coming home to him.

He was worried about his wife, true enough. But these were well past the days when they drove beaters. Ed felt pretty certain that Winnie's Monte Carlo with traction control and anti-lock brakes would bring her safely home. If not, the heated seats would keep her comfortable until someone—maybe him!—could come along and rescue her.

Of course, he'd already heard from her a few minutes ago, thanks to the cell phone he insisted she carry.

"I'm on Division. By that God mural, you know?"

"Radio says it's pretty bad."

"I don't know. Looks like God to me."

"I mean the weather, jokester. Trucks are jamming the

exits off 131."

"I think I'll be all right."

"Good. But call me, Win, if you get into trouble."

Only Ed called her Win. It was his shorthand way of letting her know that he still considered her a prize, one that he likely did not deserve. When he called her by this name, he imagined roses falling at her feet, her cheeks ready for kisses, parades down the lane.

Ed slapped his gloves together, pleased by the resulting thud, adjusted his hunting cap, and kicked the ice off the aluminum blade of his snow shovel. Everyone else seemed to look forward to the elusive Michigan spring, but Ed preferred winter. The trees exposed, you could see the neighbors better as they struggled to clear their walks, get in and out of their houses. He had a share in their lives in this way, even without saying much of anything to them.

He did not own a snow blower because it seemed a cheat. He preferred his shovel, the feel of the honest wood handle in his hands, the scrape of the blade up his shoulders. He admired the beauty of the snow. It lay before him like manna, a happy excess of blessing. With near reverence, Ed plowed a furrow down the center of the drive, a parting of the sea, a minor miracle. He had a bracing sense of being the first person on earth to bend a blade of grass, pop a grape on the tongue. Him and him alone.

Just then a billow of snow chugged toward him, intruding from the left bank of his imaginary sea.

"Hey there, neighbor!" It was Greg, wheeling his new snow blower. Greg was from Texas, had just moved into the neighborhood last fall. He'd probably huddled in his entry, scanning the skies for the first sign of a flake. Ed didn't care for the guy, his ponytail, or the odd strip of whisker above his lip the razor always seemed to miss. It could be worse, Ed figured. Greg could've called him "partner." As it was, Greg had to shout to be heard over the engine. He had a wide grin on his face. "This is really something, idn't it?"

Greg referred, Ed knew, not only to the snow, but the entire package. This was not an upscale area, but the homes were solid and well-maintained, substantial enough to fetch almost twice as much in Austin even in a depressed market. Or so Greg had said. But it did seem as if he were happy to have left the sun and higher property values behind for this chilly little corner. Win said it was cute how Greg was so happy, but Ed was put off by his stupid, dreamy joy. The guy clearly didn't know what he had gotten into. Old houses were tough. The previous owners had done their best with it, but the old Vanderstrick place had too many problems for Greg and his copy of *The Reader's Digest Guide to Flushing a Toilet.*

Greg cut the engine and stared up at the heavens as if the snowstorm, the cold wind, all of winter itself, were still more examples of things he owned. Ed wanted to tell him that his Texas ass gave him no right of ownership to anything in Michigan, particularly not the winters. Instead, he leaned forward into his shovel and said, "You gotta love a blizzard."

Ed said this with the kind of sarcasm he knew Greg would appreciate, as if Ed in fact did not love a blizzard, and the whole idea made him weary. Even so, there was something to Ed's words. Truth be told, he did love a blizzard.

"I hear you," Greg said, and licked his lips. A sliver of

fuzz glistened just above his top lip, a spot that should have been obvious to the man if he'd taken one glance in the mirror. It seemed to Ed just short of immoral.

Greg surveyed Ed's drive. "Must be what, eight inches already?"

Ed cringed. In Michigan, a person didn't talk about snow in numbers. Who cared how many inches? It was another thing for Ed to imagine Greg doing obsessively: scampering about in his home clutching a ruler, making sure everything was slightly larger than necessary.

Ed returned, "It's a big snow."

"Where's Winnie?" Greg asked. "Inside?"

Certainly, Ed knew there was a twenty-year age difference here, and that Greg had a wife of his own, Emily, but there was something between Greg and Win. Maybe it was a relief for Win to have someone close to their sons' ages around again. Their oldest had met a native on a study abroad semester in Germany and hadn't been home in seven years. The younger one was just over the border in Indiana but may as well have been overseas himself. It was best not to get too involved in their lives, Ed figured. For one, they didn't seem interested in his opinions about careers or marriage, and for two, meddling would only bring a person heartache.

For Win, Greg fit easily into the absence. She would tell Ed, "Being nice to Greg might mean that someone is being nice to our boys, so it won't kill you." Win thought the world worked that way.

Greg looked toward Ed's house hopefully, as if Win might emerge with a steaming cup of cocoa and reaffirm the canvas he imagined his new life to portray. Ed was only too happy to disappoint. "She's not here." He left it hanging, mysterious.

Greg looked up at him, quizzical, as if to say, "Aren't you worried about this? Why aren't you worried? Shouldn't a man be worried about the whereabouts of his wife on a night like this? A wife like Winnie?"

"She's on her way home," Ed said, gesturing slightly with the shovel, enough to let Greg know that Ed had a task at hand, and it was time to get back to it. Instead, another smile spread across Greg's face.

"Partner, let's get this knocked out!" and before Ed could protest, Greg had the snow blower cranked up again, spewing marble-sized chunks toward the street. There was nothing for Ed to do but watch.

No doubt about it, a snow blower moved faster than a shovel. But a shovel got to the concrete; the blower left a half-inch pack that refused to melt off the walk. As Greg finished, Ed heard the crunch of snow beneath tires behind him. Headlights lit the driveway like a stage. Ed turned in time to see Win's Monte Carlo pulling to a stop, snow scattering and melting on the warm hood. Ed poked halfheartedly at the snow left on the drive.

"My heroes," Win said when she stepped out of the car. She walked to Greg, gave him a quick hug. "Thank you, Greg. I know Ed could use the help."

"Winnie," Greg said, pausing as if he were about to relate something profound, "No problem."

In his worst moments, Ed dreamt about running Greg over with his snow blower, scattering his hippie chunks to the curb. In his best moments, Ed considered milder solutions, like building an eight-foot fence in the backyard with surrounding motion detectors.

"Ed and I are so glad you and Emily moved in," Win

said. "He'd never tell you, but his back thanks you."

There Ed stood, suddenly looking feeble next to the shovel. It hadn't been that long ago that he'd been the one shoveling what was now Greg's walk. Just last winter. The eighty-two-year-old Henry Vanderstrick never thanked him. He'd barely even nodded. And that was as it should be.

Spring came, and the trees began to obscure the houses again. Ed had to spray the crabapple trees in his backyard, to prevent fungus from ravaging the mature leaves later in the season. Greg was in his yard too, laying fertilizer in a new broadcast spreader, which Ed noticed still had the cardboard overlay with instructions for its use. Greg had probably pored over it, trying to make sure he did everything correctly not only in English but also in French and Spanish. *Cuidado, hombre!* Ed chuckled to himself. He straightened his face when Greg waved.

Ed turned off the nozzle to his sprayer. "Getting the lawn in shape?" Ed said.

Greg nodded. "I can't seem to get anything to come in here at the property line." Greg pointed to the shrubs that separated the yards. There had never been a fence there, as long as Ed knew, but he'd been seriously rethinking that. "There's these brown splotches."

Sure enough, just on the other side of Ed's nice green fescue, Greg's looked washed out and sickly.

"I'm afraid there's some kind of worm under there." Greg stared at the ground, confused.

"Yeah," Ed said, attempting to commiserate. "It's the tiny creatures that get us." Ed gestured to his crabapples. "I've got to spray these every spring to keep the fungus away."

"Fungus?" Greg asked, suddenly noticing with horror the sprayer at Ed's feet.

"Don't worry," Ed said, returning to his work. "This bug doesn't attack lawns."

Greg nodded, but his look of horror did not subside. Ed realized that Greg was silently questioning his own tools. "A sprayer? Why don't I have one of those? Where did he get his? I'd better check *Consumer Reports.* I'll bet I can find one even better."

From the corner of his eye, Ed saw Greg peering down, inspecting his lawn. He combed his fingers through the grass, as if straightening the blades might work. Then he turned the spreader upside down, as if the answer to all his problems might lie underneath.

Cuidado, hombre!

A couple of weeks later, Win invited Greg and Emily for dinner. Ed didn't put up a fight; Win had long accused Ed of not really knowing what he wanted socially. He liked the company of others to an extent, but he also wanted people to let him alone. "Maybe you just want a succession of people to stop by, nod, approve of your solitude, and then go away."

When Win smiled, her mouth opened to reveal her teeth, healthy, with a slight upward curve to the gums. Even with her lips closed, her teeth were always smirking. It was one of the things Ed loved about her, an inside joke he was always in on.

With nothing to do as Win prepared for the dinner, Ed set up his table saw in the driveway. From there he noticed Greg and Emily leave their house and begin the short walk over. He did not look up, but instead loaded another strip of wood.

As the saw spewed dust, Greg looked at the blade, mesmerized. He watched Ed feed the wood through and finish it with a guide. Ed had been doing carpentry work since he was a kid, and he made it look easy. When Ed finished ripping the wood, Emily was the first to speak.

"Getting some work done?"

"Oh, I putter a little," Ed said.

Finally, Greg broke into a grin. "That's some machine there," he said, as if a table saw were a recent technological breakthrough.

Emily stroked Greg's hair with the palm of her hand. "I wish he were that handy."

Ed was surprised at her condescension towards her husband, but Greg seemed to accept it. Emily wore old-fashioned horn-rimmed glasses and clompy shoes, purposely designed to make her look ugly. She might have been pretty, but it was impossible to tell. Ed was surprised she hadn't gone ahead and slipped on a back brace and an Elizabethan collar to complete the look.

Greg held a stringy plant as a gift. It occurred to Ed that Greg looked a little weedy himself, bristly and uneven. Texas, Michigan—he could root himself anywhere and survive. Even thrive. Greg shrugged, jostling some of the potting soil to the ground. "Maybe I *am*," he said. "Handy." Greg seemed to think he possessed hidden talents that those around him had yet to witness. "You never know."

Emily smiled at Ed as if, in fact, she did know, but she tolerated Greg anyway. Still, it seemed to Ed that Greg felt he had something to prove to his wife.

"I'd like to borrow that sometime," Greg said, indicating the saw. "I've got a couple of projects myself."

Ed made a sweeping motion with his hand, like a magician might, as if the entirety of his home were available to anyone, provided they just ask. "Take it tonight," he said.

Emily sighed, as if she were allowing her toddler just one more toy from the store, one that she knew he would never play with.

Inside, Win made a big deal about the plant, and Emily's shoes, and Greg's helping out so much last season with the snow blower. Ed wondered how long before they went back home.

Win, who always tried to encourage Ed to interact, instructed him to lead Greg on a tour of the house. "And you boys come back with an appetite."

Because he didn't know what else to do, Ed showed Greg the lighting he installed in the upstairs closets.

"Our closets are pretty dark, too," Greg said.

"When houses like yours and mine were built, people kept their clothes in chiffarobes."

Greg nodded as if he'd heard the history lesson before.

Ed pointed to the ceiling. "I nearly knocked myself out getting up to the attic."

"You do all the work yourself?"

"Yep. Just dropped a wire and plugged in the new circuit."

"New circuit? Is that up to code?"

"What do you mean?"

"Any time you put in a circuit, you're supposed to get a permit."

Ed squinted. "I've never had any problem with that."

Was the guy planning to turn him in to the city inspector? "Hey," Ed said, deciding the tour was over. "Maybe dinner's ready. Let's go check."

Ed prayed before dinner, and he noticed that Greg and Emily seemed a little uncomfortable. Let them be, Ed thought. This was his house, his food, and they were going to eat it blessed whether they liked it or not. He drew it out a little longer than usual, adding a few more broad blessings and a lengthy pause before the amen.

After Greg complimented Win on the table settings, the pork loin, the buttery rolls, and the green beans from a can, the conversation got around to the previous owners of Greg and Emily's home.

"The Vanderstricks were wonderful people," Win said.

"They kept to themselves," Ed said.

"We still get mail addressed to them," Emily said. "Lots of sweepstakes. They must have fallen for every trick in the book."

Ed cleared his throat and looked down at his plate. He didn't want to hear about anybody else's mail.

"You know they were married for fifty-eight years?" Win said.

Emily twirled her fork. "Remarkable."

"Wonder what their secret was," Greg said.

"Easy," said Ed. "Henry did everything Regina told him to."

This drew some chuckles, but Emily laughed out loud. "It's working for us so far! Right honey?"

Greg shrugged, embarrassed. "I guess." Then he turned away from his wife and looked at Win. "I can't seem to get the yard under control. I've got these viny things coming up, and I have no idea what they are."

"I think I can help you with that," Win said.

"We're also thinking of composting," Emily said, sticking a thumb towards Greg, "as soon as he figures out where to put the pile."

Emily looked to Ed like the kind of girl who married for the same reason she bought recycled paper towels. She thought Greg was eco-friendly, a choice she made with the strength of her convictions. Some people's marriages held firm on a foundation of religion; theirs was the Green Party. Someday, Ed would have to mention the snow blower to Emily, see how exactly that fume-chugger fit in with her worldview.

"How's the grass?" Ed asked.

"Not so good," Greg said.

"Worms?"

"No. I think some animal might be ruining it, or . . ." Greg lowered his voice, "Or someone is coming in at night and urinating on it."

Suddenly everyone at the table cast their eyes toward Ed. He looked at each of them separately and said, "What? Don't look at me. I've enjoyed indoor plumbing for years!"

Amid laughter, Win said, "I wouldn't put anything past you."

"Listen, if I were going to mess up your lawn to make mine look better, I'd find a much more creative way to do it. A trained mole, maybe."

Ed basked in the enjoyment he was providing at the table. He even smiled at Greg. When a person laughs at your jokes, it's hard to dislike him. By the time Emily finally thanked them for a wonderful evening, Ed was almost sorry to see them go. "Wait," he said. "The saw."

Greg refused any help. He picked it up awkwardly, so

that all the weight was on his back. As he was waddling home down the sidewalk, Ed cupped his hands to his mouth. "Don't cut your finger off!"

Win slapped Ed on the shoulder.

"What? I'm being helpful," he said with a smirk.

Greg turned and nodded in the dark. The table slipped and Ed heard the clang of metal.

Ed shook his head. "I'll never see that saw in one piece again."

"That's the price you pay . . . " Win said.

Over the course of the summer, it seemed Greg did everything he could to sabotage any hope of a friendship. First it was an invitation for Ed to join the other neighbors and pitch in for a mosquito zapper. "West Nile is a real problem," Greg said, adding, "especially for the elderly."

"Watch yourself," Ed joked.

Greg went on to say that Ed's feeder was a problem because birds were carriers. "The fewer birds around, the better."

Maybe, but Ed didn't tell him it was Win's feeder— Greg probably would have changed his tune.

Greg also mentioned that he might have seen "some kind of rat" in the sewer and would they mind getting a container for their trash? He gave Ed a can of foam sealant, directing him to use it to fill the holes in his basement. Keeps out mice, "or whatever," he said ominously, as if Ed's house were crawling with pests, the scourge of the block. Greg also suggested sharing a landscaping service to "spruce up the neighborhood." The last straw was Greg's offer to scrape, sand, and paint Ed's shutters "to match the color you're thinking of painting your house next. It's about time for that, isn't it?"

Since these requests, Ed had stopped mowing as regularly as he used to. He'd let it go a couple of weeks. Dandelions began to sprout, but instead of spraying Ed left them alone.

Finally Win asked what was wrong and he said, "Nothing. Other projects on my mind. Gotta seal up that basement, you know. Keep the neighbors happy."

Win shook her head. "He just wants to be your friend. Can't you see that?"

"He made you take down your bird feeder. He doesn't think about anyone but himself."

Win sighed. "Look out the window. How many cars do you see in the driveway?"

He didn't have to say the number. He could see that Emily's car was gone. "I suppose that means something?"

Win closed her eyes in disgust. "Emily has decided to go back to Austin for a time. That house that Greg kept talking about its value? They haven't been able to sell it. Or maybe Emily just never wanted to."

"How long has she been gone?" He'd seen that her car had been gone for a while, but he hadn't let himself think about it. It wasn't any of his business.

"Maybe a week. He didn't want me to tell you." Win went to the kitchen and brought back a dish of meatloaf.

"Me? Why? What would I care?"

Win glared at him. "That boy is in a crisis," she said. "Not that you'd see it." She opened the back door. "I'm going over there."

Ed asked what for, but the only answer he got was the door shaking in the frame. Ed considered the house around him, larger without Win. He remembered how it had gotten larger when his boys had left home. He already wondered how long she'd be gone.

That evening, Win had still not made it back home. Ed went out back, and stopped at the property line between their houses. He saw only one light on, in an upstairs bedroom. It couldn't be possible that something was going on between them. Greg was just a kid. If anything, she was reading him a bedtime story.

Ed thought of his own sons, when they were six and eight, the ages he'd enjoyed the most. They'd laugh at the funny faces he made, and they rooted for the same teams he did: Tigers, Lions, Spartans, Red Wings. He knew his kids, without even having to talk to them. As they got older, things got harder. They got interested in soccer, and video games, and other things that made no sense to him. The first time he encountered a closed door, he respected that, and walked away.

Here in the moonlight, Ed knew he was sheltered by the leafy trees that surrounded him. He did not know where his wife was. He could only guess where his sons were. He knew his house was behind him, and his two feet stood firmly on his own ground. He drew down, and felt the night under him, and he felt the release as he made zigzag patterns across Greg's lawn. He stood there a long time before turning around and walking back home.

After a couple of chilly weeks with Win and no word at all from Greg, Ed thought he had won. As always, it was better to leave people alone, and let these things blow over. They had a way of working themselves out. Then Ed heard a knock on the back door. It was Greg.

He had a towel wrapped around his left hand, and safety goggles strapped around his eyes. Sawdust clung to his ponytail and flecked the rims of the goggles. "Is Winnie here?"

"She's not. She's over at her mother's."

"Emily's not in the house, either." Greg paused. Two tiny red dots shone on his cheek. "I've got a problem," he said, looking over Ed's shoulder as if Winnie might materialize. "Can I borrow some ice?"

"I think we're all out." Ed went to the freezer, pulled out an empty tray. He turned it upside down to demonstrate.

"All right," Greg said, turning to go. He looked a little woozy, so Ed stopped him.

"What's the matter? Why do you need ice?"

Greg breathed deeply. "I cut off the end of my finger, and I was hoping to pack the nub in some ice."

Ed could see now the red in the towel was not a design but blood. "Which finger?"

"Just my pinky," Greg said, dismissive. "But it's kind of got me freaked out."

Ed dropped the tray on the floor. "Let's think here. Think." Ed clapped his hands. "Something cold." He opened the refrigerator. "Milk!"

Greg leaned in the doorway while Ed removed the carton and rummaged in the cupboard.

"Win's got some Tupperware here somewhere . . . here!" Ed produced a twelve-cup mixing bowl and emptied the milk into it. Ed pointed with the empty carton. "Go ahead. Put it in there."

Greg hesitated. "Are you sure?"

"It's what you do with a knocked-out tooth. Happened

103

to our oldest boy." Of course, those many years ago Win had been the one who knew the milk trick. It worked, too. But Greg didn't move. Frustrated, Ed slammed the carton in the trash. "You have a better plan?"

Greg looked up at him, then moved toward the bowl. He unwrapped part of the towel from his hands and shook it over the rim. The nub snagged on a loop of fabric on the towel and hovered over the bowl. Greg's eyes glazed, and it looked like he might faint.

"Don't look at it," Ed said. Ed reached out and flicked the pinky. The second time he batted the finger, it released and plopped into the milk.

Ed spilled a dozen lids on the floor, but couldn't find one the right size, so he tore off a long strip of plastic wrap. "Don't worry," Ed said, wiping a drop of sweat from his head. "I can get it really tight." He wrestled with the wrapping a moment. "See? You could bounce a quarter off that."

Greg seemed satisfied with the job and they piled into Ed's truck, Greg holding the bowl on his lap.

Ed asked, "Does it hurt?"

"Not really," Greg said. "I was hallucinating crickets for awhile . . . Hope I didn't ruin your saw."

"I'm sure it's fine," Ed said, looking ahead to the traffic. After a moment, he said, "I *told* you not to cut your finger off."

Greg blinked. "I should listen to you."

"Now you're talking."

Despite Ed's offers, Greg insisted on carrying the bowl inside the emergency room. He looked at his finger through the Glad Wrap. "It floats," he said vaguely.

Ed peeked in, nodded. The nub bobbed as Greg walked, and the milk sloshed at the sides of the bowl. Ed regarded the plastic wrap on the bowl with pride: it was holding tight. They approached the receptionist together. Greg still wore his safety goggles.

"Oh honey," the woman behind the counter said to Greg, as if he'd brought in a baby and was holding it the wrong way. "Let me have that."

She asked Ed if he was Greg's father, and he responded with a quick no. She handed a clipboard to Greg, but he just stared at it.

"Can he fill these out later?" Ed asked, but she said no.

Ed found a seat, and he did his best to just use the pen and try not to remember any of Greg's most personal information. But it was impossible not to listen. He learned that Greg did not smoke or use drugs, occasionally had a glass of wine, had asthma when he was a kid, an appendectomy when he was seventeen, and was a few years younger than Ed thought—only twenty-nine. Ed wondered how many other things he might have been wrong about.

In the waiting room, Greg began to get a little panicky. He even started to moan, drawing looks from the women behind the glass. "I can't do anything right," he said. "Emily's going to kill me."

"Take it easy. It's not like it was your whole hand," Ed said. "Look." Ed wiggled his pinky. "I hardly ever use mine. You sip a lot of tea?"

Greg just shook his head. He confessed that things had not been going well with his marriage. Emily experienced two miscarriages since their move to Michigan.

Ed wanted to tell him that what happened in his own

house, behind his own doors was his own business. But he couldn't. That door had been flung wide open, and he couldn't see a way to get it closed again.

"She's down a lot. She misses Texas."

"Maybe you should move back," Ed said, suddenly realizing maybe he could solve their problems along with his own. "To Texas."

Greg shook his head. "I can't. I've thought it through. If we move back there, she'll never have any faith in me. I gotta make my stand here." Greg stared down at his wrapped hand. "But maybe she's right. Maybe I am a screwup."

Ed tried to think what Win would do. What if Greg were his own son? What would he say then, if he had the chance?

Ed paused, took a big breath. "Look, Greg," he said. "I've been pissing on your lawn."

Greg stopped moaning and stared back at him, his head cocked. For a moment, Ed thought Greg might hit him.

"I don't know why. Maybe . . . I was jealous. Anyway, I'm sorry."

Instead of hitting him, Greg said, "You're just saying that to make me feel better."

Ed shrugged. "Take it however you want."

Greg nodded. "Thanks, partner."

Ed walked to the receptionist's window and tapped on the glass. "You'd think a guy cuts his finger off, he'd get seen a little quicker."

Instead of responding the woman said, "He's not from around here, is he?"

"What are you talking about?"

She looked over at Greg. "When he moans, he doesn't say 'oh' like a Michiganian would."

Ed wanted to tell her there was a man in pain here, that he felt sorry for her if she couldn't understand that. Instead, he just shook his head, looked her in the eye and said, "Michi*gander.*"

When the microsurgeon arrived, Ed told Greg he could wait for a while if he needed him to. A half hour later, a nurse came out and stood in front of Ed. She held the Tupperware bowl. "Does this belong to you?"

Ed shifted in his seat. "Yes."

"The girls back there saw the bowl and thought you'd brought a dish to pass."

"Is the finger okay?"

"We'd never heard of dunking it in milk, but it cleaned up just fine."

"So everything's all right? The finger's back on?"

"Oh, no. It'll be a miracle if we can reattach that finger. Even if we do, he probably won't be able to feel it, or move it like he should."

Ed considered this information. "How's he doing?"

"Fine. Great. He wanted me to tell you to go on home if you want."

"He cut that finger off with my saw."

The nurse nodded. "This could take several more hours. Really, we can call you when the time comes."

Ed stared down into the empty bowl. A couple of drops of milk remained, hugging the rim. He thought about Win. He imagined her coming home to an empty house, kitchen in a mess. He wondered where she would think he might be. She would probably check the garage first.

She would see his truck was gone. Would she think he had gone to the store? Or would she think maybe he'd done something that he'd never done before? Would she think he had driven to Indiana to see their son? Would she for a second think that? Would she for a second imagine where he was right now?

"Nah," he told the nurse. "You go back in there and tell him I'm staying." Ed motioned her back to her post. "For as long as it takes. You go tell him. Tell him I'm his ride. I'm going to take him back home."

The Spooky House

Diane has stranded Robert with the kids on Halloween. The woman who was supposed to coordinate the trunk-or-treat event at the library where she works is sick, so Diane has to go. "I've laid the costumes out. You'll have to help Clara but Elijah can manage himself." Even though Diane has spelled everything out for him, he's certain there will be one thing he won't be prepared for, and he'll be made to look like an idiot.

Diane tells him she's leaving and he asks why so early. "So I can pick up my prescription at Walgreens." Right. She's up to four medications now, all to get her chemicals balanced. "It's what they do to women," he'd said when she started the first one. "Drug them up so they can't feel anything. They made a movie about it."

They went through long, hard conversations where his only goal was to get her to either say it is, or is not, his fault. As things stand, she says it's not.

Now, she says the pills are working. She tells him, "You're sweet for worrying, but I'll know if they aren't safe." Robert is forced to face the possibility that he'd rather the pills didn't work, maybe even that they would do something horrible to her, just so he might be proven right. But that's not the way to do it, he knows. He wants Diane to feel better, even if he doesn't play a part in it.

Diane kisses the kids goodbye and reminds them of the reason that she's leaving—so all the boys and girls can get candy, not just the lucky ones like them. Robert interprets the tilt of her head to be directed at him and to mean, *You are selfish if you want me to stay home. Cooperate.*

Like so many of their friends, they'd stopped at two children. Most days, handling two was plenty, but he couldn't help thinking of the large pioneer families and how a small family still seems un-American. The worry used to be overpopulation and how the earth might not support humanity. Now it looks like there might not be *enough* people. If you listen to people predict the future, you might allow yourself to do anything.

How could he handle more kids, anyway? These days, bad or good, all fingers point at the parents. He's stopped trying to plan for success; now, the mission is to minimize the failures. He doesn't like what this night will require of him: holding a flashlight, keeping an eye on two kids who don't want eyes on them, forging the path. He will have one hand free to hold onto the three-year-old, but six-year-old Elijah will be loose. Elijah might—he's done it before, not that long ago—run into the street because his world is limited to the three inches in front of his face.

It turns out the thing to make him look stupid is Clara's stocking cap. "No! Mommy said I didn't have to wear it." The girl is dressed as some PBS character, who Clara insists "does *not* wear a stocking cap."

PBS is the only channel they let the kids watch, an hour a day at the most. Robert agrees with this rule—in fact it was his idea—but the shows they watch challenge him. Everything is designed to make the kids smart and accepting and kind. It all started in his own childhood, with Mr. Rogers. Since he's died the man's become practically a saint. But when Robert watches a small part of a rerun, he feels suffocated. The unrelenting kindness! Whatever you feel is okay! How can a person work on their flaws if they never get pointed out?

Robert finds a pair of old earmuffs for Clara to wear instead. He tells her this way she can talk to headquarters. Then he finds ones that must have been hers anyway. "Here you go," he tells her. "Bunny ears!"

"Those are yours," she insists. So they both put on earmuffs, his pink and white and wobbly, one of them crooked as if detecting the footstep of a hunter.

He leaves the porch light on and a bowl of candy on the front step. This had been Diane's idea. He was against it for a number of reasons, mainly because it advertises their absence, but she won. He tapes a note that says, "Please Take Only One. Happy Halloween!!"

Elijah is a skeleton with a long cape that death might wear. The costume seems too old for him but Diane said he insisted, so there you go. The mask is plastic and looks like the face is melting, a little like that Norwegian painting. It scares his sister, so Robert makes Elijah walk a few paces ahead.

The neighborhood is alive with children. It's joyous and gives Robert a headache. The other kids trample the lawns, laughing and screaming. Part of him disapproves, but another part of him wonders if his children should be having more fun than they are. It's so much to ask of him—an entire childhood might pass by in a single night.

Robert steers the kids away from some houses because

even though he knows the razor blade scare has been debunked, sometimes you still should follow your instincts. Diane does a presentation for parents and children every year before Halloween that reveals all sorts of vitamins and pharmaceuticals manufactured to look like candy. These younger adults, who treat Halloween like their personal holiday for the disaffected: who knows what they might distribute? Every year there are a half dozen houses that go all out with soundtracks and spiderwebs and such, and they are hard to avoid.

"Dad," Elijah says, dazzled by the canned sounds of moaning and the buzz of a group of happy children running away, "I want to go to the spooky house." Clara hangs back with Robert, but Elijah goes forward, fearless. This particular jackknob homeowner decided it would be a good idea to line the walk with paper lanterns. Robert wants to warn his son about the lanterns, but he imagines the look Diane would give him—*don't pass on your fears*—and keeps quiet.

"The candles are pretty, Daddy," Clara says, trying to talk herself out of being scared.

He squeezes her hand. "Don't get too close," he says, even though she's not moving.

The hem of Elijah's cape scrapes the sidewalk. Robert can see what might happen: the cape flips a lantern over, burns the paper. The flame will climb up the cape. It will move fast and sure. Elijah disappears into the porch.

There are probably coffins there, fake eyeballs, a bloody ax. Maybe the guy will make him take the candy from a bowl, severed hand hiding inside. Whatever. Adults who dress up, what are they searching for? Why do people choose to be monsters?

When Elijah emerges from the darkened door, Robert keeps his eyes on the lanterns. Inevitably, the boy's cape swishes out to the side, flickering one of the candles. Robert lets go of Clara's hand. "Stay here, honey," he says, and he knows if something happens to her it's because of the dangerous world we live in and the choices we have to make, and he reaches his son in three strides. He grabs the cape and flaps it to check for a flame.

"Dad, you're choking me."

"I know, son," Robert says. The cape is dark, cold. He lets the boy go and checks the lantern. For a brief moment he sees the candle as plastic, battery-powered, himself a fool. He becomes aware of his rabbit ears, stiff in the breeze. But a closer look tells him yes, he has been right all along. It *is* a real flame. He bends down and blows it out. Then he goes down the line and blows the flame from every one. He stands until the orange glow of the last wick dies, watches the next group of children walk through the wisps.

They arrive home before Diane. The candy bowl is empty, but the house is safe. He has no way of knowing if the neighborhood followed the rules of the note or if one kid just dumped everything in his bag. Robert crumples the note, tosses it in the bowl with his rabbit's ears.

Inside, the children sort their candy. Clara likes peanut butter so she gets the Reese's and gives away her caramels. They stack the Smarties like they're rolled coins. Some of them are the same color as the pills he has seen Diane sort. Gateways. Then Elijah pulls out a pair of cookies twisted in unmarked plastic wrap. Where had these come from?

"Dad, can I have these?"

"You know the rules," Robert says, and the look on Elijah's face says yes, he does, but it never hurts to try. The boy has plenty of candy, so he surrenders the cookies. Robert puts the package in his pocket.

Pointing to the candy, Robert says, "Whatever's not eaten by Thanksgiving is mine." He borrowed this particular rule from a parent he overheard at church. He likes gathering these tips. He thinks of it like plucking vegetables from a garden and bringing them to the dinner table. They're bountiful, free, and good for you, if you're willing to put in the work.

After the kids are in bed, Robert collects the wrappers from the dining room table, remembers the cocktail of feelings Halloween used to bring him in his childhood: all those houses and strange hands, those candy colors. The chill in the air. A dream, really, and part of it was the danger. The ghosts. You knew it was manufactured danger, but even manufactured danger is exciting.

Diane's pills lie waiting for her in a weekly organizer on top of the refrigerator, out of the reach of the children. He retrieves it and pops open the little hut marked with a "Tu." The lettering on one of the tablets mimics a smiley face. A little circle of happiness. Where is she, anyway? Shouldn't she have been home by now? He's made it through the night, navigated a couple of minor crises, but he's had enough. He wants Diane home, safe. He wants her back. He stares at the waiting pills, pops the lid shut.

The stranger's cookies are still in his pocket. Robert removes the wrapping, examines them. He figures they came from the paper lantern guy. Who knows what's baked inside? Arsenic. Ex-lax. Antidepressants. He sniffs one. Chocolate chip, with a faint chemical smell underneath. Probably from the plastic. A couple of crumbs fall to the floor. He takes a bite. It's not bad. He knows that the pills are not supposed to make you happy—nobody tells you that they will—they're just supposed to mask the unpleasantness.

Mask. Robert finishes the cookie and sneaks into Elijah's bedroom, careful not to wake him. The skeleton mask is upside down on the floor, the concave part of the mask that only the wearer is supposed to see. It crinkles in Robert's hands.

In the master bedroom Robert turns out the lights, slips into bed on Diane's side. Puts on the mask. The plastic edges bite into the tender skin around his ears. He will wait like this for her to return. His breath heats the inside of the mask, oppressive. The darkness and the holes for the eyes obscure his vision, but he can see well enough. This is what they both need. A little danger. Some fire. A little something for the pain.

Sitcom Mom

Dorothy has a Sitcom Mom. Sometimes her Sitcom Mom wears glittering, low-cut dresses with push-up bras that show her cleavage. She entertains important people at dinner parties. She drinks champagne. The parties begin after Dorothy's bedtime, but her mom makes sure the butler brings her a sparkling ginger ale in a champagne glass. She sips it in her room while she listens to the laughter downstairs. After dinner, her Sitcom Mom plays the piano and sings—the first song is special, to let Dorothy know her mom's thinking about her, and it lulls Dorothy to sleep.

Other times her Sitcom Mom wears cut-off jeans and white tank tops that show off her muscled arms. This is a very edgy series, even for these times. On the show, Dorothy's father is dead, so Dorothy's Sitcom Mom has to take care of her. Her mom smokes cigarettes while she shows Dorothy how to clean the family gun. Dorothy is only ten, but the family gun is kept in her reach. It's okay for her, because her mom teaches her how to use it. Dorothy's sitcom father had fought in wars in jungles. Her mom shows her how to swab the chambers so they don't rust. One episode took place at the firing range, where Dorothy wore goggles and earplugs and shot at black paper-doll men.

Dorothy's real mother—who wears a bathrobe at night and never throws a dinner party—worries about Dorothy. When Dorothy is home, she passes her hand in front of her face, her eyes go glassy, and she is no longer real Dorothy, but Dorothy on her TV show. Her mother played along for a while, but Dorothy started leaving notes that her mother and teachers found. They said things like, "Dorothy goes to secret places" and, "Won't you be sorry when Dorothy runs away?" Since then, Dorothy has been seeing the school psychologist.

Dorothy doesn't mind seeing the man—all the big stars have analysts. He appears in the credits as "Personal Assistant to Dorothy." If she feels like it, she lets her co-stars borrow him. He asks her questions, and he gets upset if she doesn't talk. Dorothy likes to play games with him. If she's quiet for too long, his ears turn red. His eyebrows go up and down when she lies to him. He tape-records every session, and just like they have reruns of her show, he can rerun the sessions whenever he wants. Dorothy is sure they'll be worth a lot of money when she gets more famous.

Dorothy stars in only the first half of the show. After her part is done, she delivers a public service message. "Parents, put your children to bed at once," she says. "The adult part of the show is about to start."

Dorothy has appeared in the second half only once, and it's her favorite episode. She puts the family gun to the temple of a burglar, and splatters his brains all over the kitchen wall. It took a long time for that episode to air. She had to go to the censors' offices and tell them that she knew they weren't brains, just ketchup and beans. And she made friends with the actor who played the burglar, a nice man getting his first big break. Then the censors said okay. Her character on the show had to pretend that the whole thing upset her a great deal, but when Dorothy watched it on TV, she laughed and laughed. After that episode ran, none of the bullies at school ever bothered her again. All she has to do is yell, "Ketchup and beans!" and all the boys run from her.

Dorothy thinks of her real school as a bother, something she has to do only because she's ten. But she loves her on-set tutor, Randa. They braid each other's hair, Randa pops popcorn, and they watch the prime-time shows. That's where Dorothy learns what she really needs to know—secret, grown-up things—about men, and women, and lipstick, and sex.

Her best friend on the show is the butler. His name is Charles, and he's British. On the first episode, after Charles told Dorothy that it wasn't his job to clean up her room, she put her right hand on her hip, cocked her head back, fluttered her eyes like she was exhausted and said, "Oh, *Chah*-les!" The line was such a hit, they have to do it every show. It's become her signature line.

Charles brings meals to her on silver platters. He wears a tuxedo, but secretly complains about it to Dorothy. Every meal, Dorothy eats blueberry yogurt because their sponsor is a yogurt company. She eats yogurt at home, too; they get cases and cases of it free. Dorothy eats it from a silver bowl. She likes to put two blueberries in a yogurt blob, and make a blob face out of it. She pretends they're people that bother her—her teacher Mrs. Arnold, bullies at school, the psychologist. When she pops the berries on her tongue, they can't look at her anymore.

Dorothy's real father—like on the show—isn't around anymore. He divorced her mother when Dorothy was only three years old. He sends her two gifts a year: a thirty-dollar gift card on her birthday, and a fifty-dollar gift card at Christmas. Her mother says he has no real home or address, so Dorothy thinks he could be a screenwriter. When she was seven, on Father's Day, she remembers a phone number written on a scrap of paper. She pressed the buttons as her mother called the numbers. The connection was fuzzy. It might have been a flip phone. He said, "I bet you don't even remember what I look like." All she could think to say was "Happy Father's Day" a second time.

Dorothy loves her director. His name is Girard, but Dorothy calls him Gerry. No one else gets to. He carries an old-timey megaphone and yells at everyone, but not Dorothy. He calls her Twinkle, because she's his biggest star. Dorothy has her own dressing room with her nickname on it written in glittered gold. Gerry has to knock before he can come in. Even her real mom would have to knock, if she came to the set.

Once, for a week, her mother didn't let Dorothy watch television. The psychologist said, right in front of Dorothy, "Television encourages the fantasy." So Dorothy played TV Dorothy for the entire week, and she left lots of notes. Finally, TV privileges were returned.

Her real mother doesn't like Dorothy to go to the show, so she has to sneak away to the set. Sometimes, when her mother thinks Dorothy's going to the street corner to catch the school bus, Dorothy really gets in a limousine that takes her to the studio.

Dorothy doesn't like it when she has to go to her real school. Usually, she plays by herself at recess. For a while two of the other girls, Tanya and Lacy, tried to play with her. Dorothy let them have parts in the show as extras, but they finally got tired of Dorothy being the star all the time. They didn't understand it was *her* show.

The boys tease her. They say she talks to herself, that she's nutty. There's only one boy who doesn't make fun of her. His name is Thomas. He won't talk to her at all. He doesn't talk to anyone. Sometimes she has to kick him just so he'll notice her, but then he runs away. Gerry says not to worry, that most child actors are too temperamental to work with—Dorothy is one of a kind.

She's already had to change homeroom teachers once. Dorothy thinks Gerry must have arranged it for her. She can just see him talking to the principal. She bets he used the megaphone, right in the principal's ear.

"You don't see this little star of mine playing pattycake children's games. She's almost grown up! That teacher of hers is just too mean. You need to find a teacher who respects my Twinkle's talent."

But Mrs. Arnold hasn't been much better. She sends Dorothy to the office every time she says anything about rehearsal or studying her lines, or anything about the show. Even when Dorothy does her work, Mrs. Arnold scowls. Once, after Dorothy turned in a homework exercise identifying facts and opinions, Mrs. Arnold called her to the front.

"Why have you labeled everything an opinion, Dorothy?" Dorothy didn't answer, so Mrs. Arnold made Dorothy's real mother come to the school. Dorothy sat in the hall and listened.

"*People can't live without water.* That's a fact," said Mrs. Arnold. "*Most people in the world live in China. The United States is an independent nation.* All facts! I'm afraid this little girl really lives in a world without facts."

The psychologist brought the worksheet to their session. They'd never done homework together before. Dorothy thought it best to keep quiet. The tape player whirred, recording nothing, and his ears got redder and redder.

Since then, Dorothy's real mother is home every day when Dorothy gets out of school. She works for a travel site, offering vacations to other people. Dorothy feels sorry for her because she never gets to go anywhere herself.

Dorothy goes lots of places because her Sitcom Mom is a pilot. They have an airstrip in the backyard for long trips, and they have a helicopter for short trips in town. Her Sitcom Mom likes to fly to England to shop for jewelry for both of them. Charles has taught them both to speak with a British accent when they're over there, so they don't sound like they're from America. When they go to Japan, her mom can speak the language, but Dorothy can't, so she just purses her lips and silently bows to everyone.

She hasn't gone anywhere lately because every afternoon, for half an hour, Dorothy and her real mother do an activity together. Sometimes they play a game, like Old Maid, or make a collage, or one time they made chocolate chip cookie dough, but ate it all before putting it in the oven. Today, her real mother says, "What time does the show start?"

Dorothy doesn't know whether to answer or not. "I

don't know."

"Can I have a part in the next show?"

Dorothy can feel her heart beating faster. She thinks for a minute and says, "If I had two mothers, it'd be a different kind of show." Actually, her Sitcom Mom would probably yell at her real mother. Or just ignore her. Maybe she'd laugh at her.

"No, you can't be on the show."

Dorothy is not stupid. She has an active imagination, and that is a very good thing. Sometimes she wishes she could tell the kids at school this, but they would never believe her. She is thinking this as she is handing out milk. It is the first time she's been chosen as milk monitor, and Dorothy wants to show Mrs. Arnold that the choice was long overdue. There's never been a milk monitor like Dorothy before. She's dressed in clothes so out of fashion that they're in fashion, but none of the other kids are with it enough to realize. Or admit it. She pirouettes, flips her skirt, bounces her braids, and deposits a half-pint on silent Thomas's tray.

"You're a fake," Thomas says, never looking up from the table.

Dorothy freezes, one braid in front of her shoulders, one behind. "Are *you* talking to *me?*" Dorothy has heard this line before, and it occurs to her that it's a very grown-up thing to say.

"Yep." Thomas puckers his lips around his Krazy-Straw. "You're not a star. Everybody knows it."

Dorothy puts her hands on her hips. "Prove it."

"I don't have to. You're not on TV."

Dorothy has heard this argument before. She closes

her eyes like the challenge doesn't affect her. "I'm on a channel you don't get."

"We have a satellite. I know all the channels, and you're not on any of them."

"It's not nice to call someone crazy," Dorothy says.

"I didn't. I just said you're not a star. You might think you're one, but you're not."

"Maybe," Dorothy says, hesitant, then brightening. "But you don't ever talk to anybody," she said, "and you talked to *me.*"

One day, when Dorothy comes home from school, the television is gone.

"What happened?" Dorothy asks her mother, stunned.

"I sold it. I think we can do without it."

Dorothy stands, lips parted.

"I bought some orange construction paper," her mother says. "We can cut pumpkins for the door."

"I don't feel like it."

"That's okay. You just tell me when you do." Her mother begins working the scissors around the outside of the paper.

Dorothy pauses. This just proves her mother doesn't understand, not anything. "This won't work, you know," Dorothy says. "It's not just about the TV."

"No?" Her mother continues cutting.

Dorothy frowns. It's about so much more than TV. It's about her whole life, how it's not good enough. And it's not even that she's ordinary. She's *less* than ordinary. She's a freak, and unless she does something about it, she'll stay this way her whole life. Lacking in excitement, lacking in popularity, lacking in glamour. Just lacking. Like her mother. "Maybe you'll see that," Dorothy says, storming off, "*Even*tually."

Having no television will change her life at home, but it shouldn't affect her show. After all, the script never even mentions a television. Dorothy will have to speak with Gerry.

Gerry looks concerned. "The show's in trouble. Production costs are up, and we're losing sponsors."

"Not the shoe people?" Dorothy endorses shoes for a jump rope company. A lightning bolt sizzles across the sides of the shoes when she jumps.

"They're the only sponsor left."

Dorothy is relieved until Gerry says, "The show is getting stale. It needs a plot twist."

Dorothy knows all about ratings, sweeps weeks. Anytime a show falters, a change has to be made.

"I could pretend to . . . I could run away from home."

"No, there has to be a new character. A new baby for your mom."

"What about *me*?" She wishes her Sitcom Mom would help her negotiate, but she's far too busy.

"You're getting too old," Gerry says. "The Charles line isn't cute anymore."

On Saturday morning, Dorothy's real mother is asleep. Dorothy has gotten up early, braided her own hair, and tied it with a pink ribbon. She walks down the familiar streets of her neighborhood, the sun low in the morning sky. "This is a great day to shoot," says Gerry, all smiles, pretending yesterday's discussion never happened. The opening shot is the most important, and today Dorothy knows the lighting doesn't get any better. Her face is in just the right amount of shadow, her green eyes sparkling, her cheeks scrubbed rosy. She'll teach them whose show it is.

She begins to skip, humming the theme song to her show under her breath. It doesn't have any words, but the tune is upbeat, a cross between the themes to *Sesame Street* and *Married . . . With Children.* The opening montage changes every week. This time, Gerry thinks she looks good just skipping on the sidewalk, humming the song herself.

The title of this episode is "Dorothy Rebels." She must pretend to be jealous of the new baby. She must do something bad, for attention.

One of the little neighbor boys rides down his walkway on a bright red tricycle. She can't be bad to littler kids, she decides, because that would make her unsympathetic. Dorothy puts her hands on her knees, cocks her head at him, smiles, and says, "And what's your name, little boy?"

"My name's Robby. You're Dorothy. I know you already."

"Oh. Well, do you need any help today?"

"No, but I'm gonna run over you if you don't get out of my way. I'm a ten-ton locomotive."

Dorothy shakes her head and looks over her shoulder into the camera. "Kids today—just won't listen to anyone trying to help them," she says, and sells it with a wink.

Dorothy finds a smooth rock on the sidewalk. Gerry thinks it would be a good idea if they had a sequence where she plays hopscotch. "We can reach a bigger market for the shoes if people see they're good for hopscotch, too."

He tells her to just pretend there are hopscotch squares on the sidewalk, and they can add them to the film later.

Dorothy doesn't do it right the first time, so Gerry makes her do it again. "Dorothy skipping hopscotch, take two," she says, and smacks her hands together like a clapboard.

As the day wears on, Gerry's mood gets testy. Nothing Dorothy does pleases him. If she does the hopscotch right, the camera is never at the right angle, so she has to do it over and over, to get every angle. He says they might use the footage for some promos. Anyway, Dorothy doesn't mind. Even though she usually doesn't like a kid's game like hopscotch, it's fun to pretend like she's still a kid, for the show. After the baby comes, she'll practically be an adult.

Dorothy keeps walking, and hopscotches every now and then. A drop of sweat falls on Dorothy's eyelash, and Gerry stops rolling. "It won't do for our star to sweat on camera," says Gerry. She has almost forgotten about being bad, but Gerry hasn't. "Come on, Dorothy—what are you going to do?" The sun is high—Dorothy's been walking a long time, and they've lost the golden light.

Then, from inside a house on her right, Dorothy hears a shrill laugh. It's a white house with hard, black iron grating around an enclosed porch. The house is made of wood, and the paint is peeling at the seams. Dorothy has never seen this house before. She checks the street sign— it's still her street, but nothing looks like it does in her neighborhood, and she hears the laughing again, only this time she's not sure; it might be crying. She sees an arm pass behind the window, and a man looks out, a thin man in an undershirt.

"This is your chance," Gerry whispers.

Dorothy is scared, but she walks to the man's door. This must be the kind of story that usually happens in the second half of the show, when she's in bed. But she has to do it, to save her show. To save her life, maybe. She knocks on the door.

The man waves curtains from the windowed door. Dorothy's mouth goes dry as she watches his hairless arms. Her lips tremble as he opens the door.

"Hello?" Brown spots wrinkle into his scalp.

Dorothy braces herself. "I'm lost," she says. This is the first episode she's ever talked to any stranger but a policeman. Then she adds, "And I'm all alone." She shivers with these words and closes her eyes, thinking, *If he asks me in, I'll go, and if he does unspeakable things to me, it will be his fault, not mine, and I'll be able to tell my Sitcom Mom, and everything will be okay.*

The man rubs his chin and shifts his head, like he's looking for cameras. "Well . . . I can try and call your momma. Do you know your phone number?"

The man smells like moss. Through the door, the house looks messy: advertisements on the floor, a dingy rug, a couch with a missing cushion. She knows—even without Gerry telling her—that if she is to save her show, no matter the consequences, she must go to that couch. A real star would do it. It's her responsibility.

But she can't move. She begins to cry. The man stands with the phone in the air, still waiting for direction. Dorothy holds her arms out to him, and sobs, "Please."

The wonk-wonk of the open line signal comes on the phone and the man presses the off button. "I'm sorry, but you can't really be in here. A guy's got to look out for himself these days." The man looks around. "You sure you're alone?"

"No!" Dorothy yells, and runs away from the house,

so fast she can't feel her arms and legs.

"Wait," the man calls, but Dorothy keeps running, farther from home, ashamed of herself like never before. She doesn't even know how to be bad.

She runs until she can't hear the man anymore. Breathless, she ends up in front of a corner grocery store. Pumpkins are stacked by the side of the store, and Dorothy sits on one and rests. She can still smell the moss.

"I wish I were home," Dorothy says, but she doesn't remember how to get back. What happened to Gerry? He probably gave up on her and wrapped for the day. If her Sitcom Mom knew where Dorothy was, she'd whiz over in the helicopter and drop down a rope ladder. But she's not here. Not even that stupid Charles is here. Dorothy has never felt more deserted. She thinks of the designs she would cut into her pumpkin if she were home with her mother.

As she imagines herself safe at home, she thinks she has probably gotten what she deserved. No real star would act the way she did. She doesn't deserve her own show.

Then, she feels a hand on her shoulder. She looks up into the face of her real mother. Instead of an action tank-top her mother wears a cable-knit sweater, and instead of a helicopter she came in their green minivan, but still the similarity is striking. "Just like my Sitcom Mom," Dorothy says.

"No, honey," her mother says, guiding her into the van. "This is real."

The episode "Dorothy Rebels" marked the last for Dorothy—her show has been cancelled. Sometimes she misses Gerry and Charles, and especially her Sitcom Mom, but she knows she can't think about them anymore. Her mind isn't safe.

She's made friends—a real friend—with Thomas at school, and even Mrs. Arnold is nice to her now. The television is back in the den, but Dorothy can only watch it with her mother. She explains the prime time shows to Dorothy. Now she gets to stay up an hour later.

"I love you, my best girl," her mother says. She lets Dorothy wear lip gloss sometimes, and says when Dorothy grows up, she can be anything she wants.

"Anything?" Dorothy asks.

"Whatever you want."

Dorothy doesn't answer, but a desire worms to the front of her brain. *Yes,* she thinks, dreaming of the way real life can be: *I will be a star.*

School Conferences at
Christ the Redeemer Middle School

"Am I late?"

A custodian is busy collapsing tables in one half of the gym. Near the stage, a single table remains. A chubby, dark-haired man you do not recognize sits behind it. He wears the colors of the school, green and white. You think he might be a coach, but not one of the good coaches.

"Depends. What were you hoping to find?" The man arranges papers in front of him, in haphazard stacks. Some of the papers have edges so worn they might be years old.

"My wife sent me. It's about our son. I'm not really sure he's going to make it through the year," you admit. Your voice echoes, and you're grateful there are no other parents still here.

The man nods. He's heard this before. He massages the collar on his shirt, which has curled in the wrong direction. It points in the right direction for a moment before gradually returning to its original curl. "Some kids won't," he says.

You tell him your son's name, even though he hasn't asked, and his head moves in a way that might signal recognition. "Look, he's a smart kid. You know that."

The man's eyelids quiver.

"He just can't handle the homework."

"Who can?" the man says.

Your neck relaxes. "So you know what I'm talking about? The kid goes to school all day, then he comes home and has four more hours of work left. That's more than my work week!"

"It's in the air of this place," the man says.

The air smells faintly of stale popcorn. The dingy floor inside the concession stand pops into your head, all the fundraising candy bars you've taken to the office to sell. "We've put a lot into this school," you say, not meaning that you expect to be treated like an investor necessarily, but that you've made quite an investment, so you say, "We've made quite an investment in this school," and you're instantly sorry for the way that sounds.

The custodian, finished with the tables, has moved on to push-brooming the floors. The broom head, matted with clots of dust, leaves a contrail of sediment behind.

"Look, you don't owe me anything," you say. "It's just . . . He does great on the standardized tests. Maybe that's enough? Maybe he could finish out the year at home? We home school him, let him read the good stuff, you know? None of this . . . " You stop yourself. "You know, we'll do a good job with him."

"You take him out," the man fans the fingers of his hand, "he's gone forever."

You wonder what he means by this but you think maybe he gets it, he knows how serious this is. You think of what might happen when you come home. "Everybody is counting on me to get some answers. You gotta help me out."

The man thumbs the papers in front of him, comes

across one that interests him. He raises his eyes to you. "You could fill out this form."

He spins it around so you can read it. "Application for Transfer," it says at the top, then on the second line it says, "of Burden." The only other marking on the paper is a line for a signature.

"Burden? Is that in this district?"

"It's not a school."

You read it again. "This can't be what it says. How can a burden be transferred?"

"It's an application," he says.

You look behind you. The gym ceiling crowds in on you. If you don't sign this paper, you'll have nothing to bring home, nothing to report. You're tired of reporting nothing. You're tired of being ineffective. You ask for a pen.

"What am I signing?" you ask.

"There are no terms," the man says.

"Will this help my son?" you ask. "Will it take his burden away?"

The man leans back in his chair. It's one of those gray folding chairs whose metal rubs bones as part of its job. "This isn't for him."

"Then who is it for?"

You touch the paper. The corners are rounded, as if it's been through the laundry. This form is yours, you realize. This is all about you. You click the pen open. "Who sees this?" you ask. He waits for you to sign before answering.

"Nobody," he says, and slides the form into a manila folder marked 3RD PERIOD.

After signing, you feel the same. A little better, maybe,

but mostly the same. "This is a nice pen," you say. Everything else at this school is junk, but that pen. A nice, smooth feel to it.

"It's the little things," the man says, "that keep us going," and his thumb uncurls his collar one more time.

The Baptist

"Dear God," Reverend Kenneth Hall says, only half praying, as he reads the obituary of his fourth grade teacher, Brenda Hampton. She died of a heart attack at the age of forty-three. Such shocking news—usually, someone would wake him in the night, especially considering an event as tragic as this. But, after all, she wasn't a member of his congregation; she attended the other Baptist church in town.

Kenneth was a little in love with Mrs. Hampton. He would find any excuse to raise his hand, just so she would come to him and bend down in front of his desk, close enough for him to smell her perfume—a hint of tropical fruit that he still associated with womanhood. When Mrs. Hampton leaned over to inspect his work, her scarf pooled on the top of his desk. Kenneth now recognizes that her wardrobe of scarves—tied in bows covering her chest— was designed to de-emphasize her shapely figure. Kenneth reads the age again. Forty-three. He does the math—she was only twenty-four when he first knew her. The younger the death, the harder it is to accept, as if a young heart were a promise from God. For it to fail so soon seems a betrayal.

Fourth grade was a big year for Kenneth. It marked the year he got baptized, and also the year he first saw a woman's breast. The first was due to his religious family, the second thanks to Jon Fenster, resident hoodlum of his class. The proximity of these two events is linked inextricably in Kenneth's memory, as if one couldn't have happened without the other.

Whenever asked about the moment that called him to the ministry, Kenneth traces it to his baptism, the event that shone so brightly ahead in the life of a ten-year-old from a Baptist family. *Baptism*—the word itself has magic, the eponymous event of his faith.

The rite still holds magic for Kenneth; he includes it as a key element in his own ministry, devoting the first Friday of every month to a special service for baptisms. The church has responded with enthusiasm; families appreciate a weekend activity they can share with their children, who never fail to be fascinated at the sight of anyone, especially adults, being dunked in water. He calls it Family Life Night, appropriate because this is the moment for believers to be washed of their sins and accepted into the family of God.

As Kenneth looks back on his own baptism, he realizes that Mrs. Hampton figured in the event, too. On the brink of acceptance into this new family of believers, Kenneth remembers imagining Mrs. Hampton, with her fresh blond features and heavenly perfume, as his new mother— the wife of God.

Even though the ceremony was held on a Sunday morning, Kenneth considers the previous Friday as the real beginning. When Kenneth went to hang his coat in the fourth-grade classroom, he found Jon Fenster and two of his buddies hidden in the coat closet, giggling. They bulged in their winter coats, in a way Kenneth is sure he'd find comical now, tiny child astronauts, waddling in gravity-deprived sluggishness. But at the time, Kenneth saw Fenster as a tough guy, whose coat made him seem old and burly.

Kenneth asked, "What's going on?"

The giggling stopped, and Fenster stuffed his hand in his pocket. Fenster wasn't talking, which was probably a smart move. Kenneth, the model student, was an outsider to this gang.

"You'll tattle," said one of the boys.

Kenneth remembers this line, amused. His childhood personality has persisted into adulthood; he has always been the arbiter of right and wrong. But instead of tattling, in the dark corner of that coat closet, with a desire to belong, he made a promise. "I won't tattle," he said, committing himself to the side of wrong. The hairs in his nostrils pricked, electric with the sense of evil.

"Fenster found some cut-up *Playboys*."

Kenneth had seen the magazine before—in Ridley's Drugstore on the other side of town—beckoning from the back shelves of the newsstand. He'd never seen past the cover, but he imagined that every page pictured women desperately naked, old and withering like the prostitutes he saw played on TV. "Where'd you find them?" Kenneth asked, stalling.

"Out by the dumpster."

"Behind the *school?*"

Kenneth occupied himself with speculation, what he considered a superior position. Why would anyone put a magazine in the school dumpster? Conspiracies raced through his mind—maybe someone was watching, waiting to bust whoever picked them up. He also thought that Fenster just might be tricking him.

"So, you wanna see?" Fenster asked.

"All right," Kenneth said wearily, to let them know he wasn't fooled. Of course, even if Fenster did have pieces from the magazine, they were probably cut so small as to be indistinguishable. Fenster removed his hand from his pocket, a glossy paper pinched in his mitten. He spread open in his palm a triangle of paper, and presented it to Kenneth. Inscribed inside the sharp edges was a round, tan breast that looked soft and young but at the same time adult, forbidden. A helpless lock of brown hair cupped the left side of the breast. Immediately Kenneth knew that even though he consciously had expected to see either nothing, or confetti-sized bits of paper, deep down, this was what he had wanted to see all along.

Before Kenneth could form an image of the woman in the picture, he felt Mrs. Hampton's hand on his shoulder. "Boys, it's time to take your seats." As he saw the disapproval in Mrs. Hampton's eyes, he knew she had seen him, and he shivered with the knowledge of what lay concealed behind her scarf.

That moment drove a wedge between him and Mrs. Hampton. He couldn't call her to his desk after that. He had betrayed his new mother, and would always be an outsider in the family of God.

The following Sunday, as Kenneth prepared for his baptism, the image of the amputated breast still floated in his mind. He knew he had sinned, but he hoped the ceremony would redeem him. In Sunday School that morning, even though half of his classmates had already been baptized, Kenneth was the star. The whole lesson was about baptism, and he stood as a shining example of the dutiful believer.

When the main service started, Kenneth waited in the wings. He folded his dress clothes on a chair, and changed into swim trunks and a tee shirt. He felt naked and ashamed, vulnerable.

When the reverend—Pastor Rick the kids called him—came to say it was almost time, even he wore a tee shirt. Kenneth didn't realize it then, but looking back, the pastor's casual attire seemed to cheapen the event, defile it. When Kenneth performs the baptismal services now, both wear a white ceremonial robe.

Kenneth waited at the edge of the baptistery for the music to stop. He saw Pastor Rick already in the water, his legs rippling weakly. Pastor Rick motioned for Kenneth to come beside him, then took a microphone from its stand.

"Better be careful with this," he said. "We just want to *talk* to God today; we don't want to *see* him." Kenneth had seen films in school with cartoon characters electrocuted when a blow dryer splashed into the bathtub. Danger revealed itself tantalizingly above the water in the form of that microphone, God's right hand. When the microphone slipped into the water, as Kenneth was sure it would, God would save Pastor Rick, but not Kenneth— he had looked at a naked breast.

Pastor Rick explained the ritual for the congregation, though everyone there knew that baptism symbolized the washing away of sin. So Pastor Rick turned it into a joke, alluding to the difference between immersion and a sprinkle. "As Baptists, we're dunkers. We're going to put

Kenny all the way under," he said, turning to Kenneth, "Because we want *all* of you to get to heaven." This drew laughter from the crowd. Kenneth conjured a comic but still grisly vision of heaven, filled with the disembodied heads of Catholics and Methodists. Still, the joke was effective, and he has stolen it for his own sermons.

Then, as they had rehearsed earlier, Pastor Rick was supposed to ask Kenneth if Jesus lived in his heart. Instead, he threw him a curveball: "Tell us, Kenny, what has God done for you?" Kenneth's mind raced. He knows now that the question was unfair—we don't get to heaven by our deeds, so we shouldn't hold God to such a test, either. But as a ten-year-old boy, Kenneth felt the responsibility fall directly on his shoulders to answer the question correctly. *What has God done for me?*

Kenneth had been desperately trying not to do anything against God; he hadn't thought of *God* as doing anything for *him.* Kenneth thought of the "blessings" his family talked about—*My, how God has blessed us*—but could only think of their mealtime prayer. *Thank you for the bounty before us.* Kenneth looked at the expectant faces. He sees the same faces in his own congregation now, tiny birds baring bottomless stomachs, beaks wide and sprung like bear traps. Finally, he squeaked, "Sometimes, when I have a stomach ache at school, God makes me feel better." Even as he said it, his voice amplifying in his ears, Kenneth knew the answer was woefully inadequate. As a child, he was sure that anything real could be confirmed by words. He had been asked to articulate his faith, and he had failed.

Now, he knows that faith cannot be explained, but it took long years of prayer for him to understand this. The rest of the baptism moves through Kenneth's memory as if it all occurred underwater. The pastor perched the microphone on the edge of the baptistery, held Kenneth by the left wrist and behind the neck, and Kenneth felt hands not cold but cool, just enough of a temperature difference to raise a question, and he closed his eyes, not to pray, but in hopes of escaping to sleep. A fatigue had come over him, presenting itself in his body as a tangible intruder as soon as Kenneth finished speaking the words that had exhausted himself of the one mystery that, until then, had protected his faith: silence. He had exposed himself as a sinner, as unworthy of baptism as Jon Fenster. Kenneth felt his body tip back into the cool hands of Pastor Rick, *I baptize you,* his body assenting into the water, displacing faith, giving himself over to doubt *in the name of the Father, and of the Son, and of the Holy Ghost.*

When the inevitable sizzle from the electrified microphone never occurred, Kenneth assumed God had spared his life for one reason: to amend the great sin of being baptized in a state of doubt. To do this, he knew he must witness to lost souls. Naturally, the person who needed God the most was Jon Fenster. Everything about Fenster, even the lack of an "h" in Jon, made him seem sinister, as if his name itself were missing its soul. On Monday at first recess, Kenneth sought him out.

"Hey," Kenneth said, hoping his smile conveyed his new holiness.

"Hey, yourself," Fenster said, exposing one of his front teeth. Its tip looked brittle, as if stained with liquid paper.

"Whatcha doing?"

Fenster's hands were deep in the pockets of his coat. Kenneth knew Fenster sometimes sneaked a cigarette at recess.

"What the hell is it to you?"

Kenneth felt the power of God shudder through him. The moment for witnessing had arisen, and he seized it. "You shouldn't cuss, you know."

Fenster returned a blank look.

"God doesn't like it."

Suddenly, Fenster broke into a smile. Kenneth was surprised to see the power through him work so immediately.

"I know what you want," Fenster said.

Maybe I have touched his conscience, Kenneth thought.

Fenster pulled a handful of the cut-up pictures from his pocket. "Here's something God *does* like."

When Kenneth saw the pictures, he couldn't speak. His resolve wilted. Fenster knelt on the ground, and Kenneth huddled next to him, blocking the wind. They spread the slices of naked flesh before them on the ground—breasts, backsides, the mysteriously bearded crotches—but no faces. For Kenneth, they were all pieces of the same puzzle, whose solution held the key to understanding what might face him in the next life, which was not heaven, whose distance seemed suddenly unreachable, but the palpable promise of adulthood, spread before him like a banquet.

When attending seminary, Kenneth slept with one woman, on two occasions. Yes, he has since asked forgiveness, both of God and of the woman, even though he loved her. He asked forgiveness because the sex had nothing to do with love, and he blames it on the wounds he received from that display on the elementary school playground, that offered desire to him as an emotion to be butchered.

Fenster got expelled late into the school year, and then his family moved away. They never spoke after that recess. Fenster still resides in a part of Kenneth, though. A failure, a lost soul. Kenneth sometimes wonders what happened to him, but more than that, he wonders: did Fenster really know what Kenneth wanted that day, before Kenneth weakened and showed his sinful heart?

Shortly before Family Life Night, Kenneth makes final preparations. He overhears people in the foyer who have just arrived from Mrs. Hampton's funeral: ". . . a shame," and, "fortunately . . . summer . . . her students would have been devastated." He considered attending, but decided he couldn't face her, even in death.

Like the other services, this one will consist of three hymns and a prayer, followed by the baptisms. Two are scheduled for tonight: a heavy man in his forties, and a boy twelve years old. Kenneth meets them both in the changing area. As the three of them stand in their white robes, they look like members of a bizarre graduating class.

"Who wants to go first?" Kenneth asks.

"I will," volunteers Harold, the older man. "I suppose I've waited long enough."

Kenneth smiles, trying to ease the man's nerves. "No need to be embarrassed. We're all the same age in the eyes of God." Kenneth gives both of them their cues, then leaves them so he can pray in solitude.

Lord, your will through my body, he prays in his darkened office. *Let my eyes be on you.*

When the last hymn is sung, Kenneth is waiting in the water of the baptistery as the curtain pulls back. He turns and motions for Harold to join him. Harold looks like a marshmallow in his white robe. Harold told him that he was afraid Kenneth wouldn't be strong enough to lift him back out of the water. "Relax," Kenneth told him. "It's all in the rhythm. Let the water push you back up."

Kenneth wades with Harold toward the microphone, cradled in its stand at the front of the baptistery. "Harold's a little nervous about all this," Kenneth says. "He came up to me and said, 'Pastor, are you sure I have to go all the way under?' So I explained to Harold that Baptists are dunkers because we want to make sure *all* of him gets to heaven." Harold shakes with laughter, and Kenneth puts his arm around him. He can feel the tension lift from Harold's shoulders.

"Do you believe in the Lord Jesus Christ as your savior?"

When he nods yes, Kenneth wastes no time in performing the office, tips him backward easily, then, just as he begins to rise to the surface, Harold's body stops, as if a hand were holding him under. Kenneth bends his legs for leverage, pushes Harold further down, then stands and yanks as hard as he can. Harold's face emerges, smiling as if nothing has gone wrong. "Praise God," Kenneth says, genuinely relieved.

Harold exits the baptistery to warm applause, robe clinging to his round frame. The boy waits on the steps. When Kenneth beckons to him, the boy smiles, exposing brittle white teeth.

Kenneth's mind spins back to the playground, to Fenster, to Kenneth's self-betrayal. The water squeezes Kenneth's body, laps around his chest. Kenneth grabs the boy, more tightly than he should, and leads him into the water. *Father, let me show this boy. Let me show him my heart.*

Kenneth wades toward the microphone, hesitates, then reaches for it. He pulls the wire directly over the boy's head, then checks his face—no sign of fear. Kenneth turns to the congregation.

"I want all of you to pray with me tonight and trust the Lord that this microphone doesn't zap us both." The congregation laughs, and the boy smiles weakly. Kenneth feels a power surging through him, guiding him toward a once-traveled path. Kenneth wants the boy to feel the power.

As if following a script, Kenneth says, "Tell me, what has God done for you?"

He offers the question just as Pastor Rick offered it to him years before. The hum of the microphone vibrates through the church.

The boy, unflappable, responds, "He has made my life complete."

Kenneth takes the boy by the back of the neck and thinks about the cleansing water, how youth really is no promise, and as he feels the scissor-thin bones of the young boy that cut the heart from his teacher, sending the flat triangle of her heart unbaptized into the crinkling fires of Hell, Kenneth leans the boy back and does to him what he should have done to Fenster long ago—ushers him out of this world and into a new one.

The Griefbearer

We didn't know what to do with our grief. There was so much sickness in that time, so much death. Bodies were buried shoulder to shoulder, reminding us of our daily grief. Something had to be done.

The first was a volunteer, one who offered to bear our grief for us. This griefbearer was righteous, a young woman of only fourteen. We would bring her our burdens and she would take them. She knew each of our loved ones by name, and she grieved the loss not just of their names but of their gestures, the accents of their bodies.

The woman bore this living grief bravely. She walked among us every day and we saw the bend of her back, low enough to let us know she was doing her job.

We were lightened.

Because she walked among us, we could gather food, chop wood, pour life into our remaining loved ones. The arrangement succeeded until some felt the first griefbearer had borne too much, so a young man was compelled into service.

At first, he was eager to learn. The old griefbearer tried to teach him how to bear our grief since doing so did not come naturally to him. She must have been a good teacher because soon enough, many felt he was just as good at his job as she was, perhaps better.

When he walked through the town, he held his back upright. We trusted he bore these new griefs, but he carried them as if they were nothing. You couldn't believe the joy we felt! Those who had no one to grieve longed for a loved one to die, just to experience the consequent elation of relieving the burden.

Only one of us suspected something was wrong: the old griefbearer.

She still walked among us, back bent. She shook her head and conveyed the danger we were in, but we didn't listen and one day, the young man disappeared.

The girl told us what she had been telling us all along: The boy never listened to us, never knew our loved ones. He had not been bearing our grief. She had. She was the only righteous griefbearer, and all our grief flowed to her. If she didn't get help, we would be back to bearing our own grief. And this time, it would be harder than before.

But the ones whose grief had been borne by the boy were as happy as ever. New mourners ignored the girl and continued giving their burden to the boy, even long after he'd disappeared.

The girl remained, her back lowering daily. She said we had lost something when we'd given our grief to her, that one person was never meant to bear so much. One day, we would feel this loss, she said. She spoke in such an old-fashioned language that we were embarrassed for her. Sad for her, really, for not understanding what it meant to live a life without care. To truly be free.

Cleaning House

I just bought my first house, in Phoenix. It's old, but built on a solid foundation. Feels like a step in the right direction after living in a trailer in Oklahoma with Celia. There, every dark cloud threatens to drill a tornado into your possessions, upending your entire life. I managed to avoid the dangers of the climate, but the real tornado, I found, was Celia herself. She's gone now, and I'm miles away, too old to live in a trailer anymore.

The guy who sold me the house is a bachelor too, close to my age of twenty-seven. He's invested in a gold mine near Prescott. No kidding, he's going to live *at* the mine. Good luck to him. Meanwhile, I'm cleaning his filth from my house. Buried underneath, I may unearth something of my own.

I've only been here a couple of months. My seven-year B.A. in archaeology has gotten me, of all things, a job as a systems analyst for the largest bank in town. I fudged my resume—I only have a minor in computer science. I blew some smoke during the interview—fiddled with their system, pulled up functions they didn't know existed. Computers come easy to me. They work in a pattern my mind comfortably falls into.

Celia had no patterns. For example, the first semester we lived together she took: a jewelry class, Modern Dance, Fencing, an upper-level British Empiricists class that I have no idea how she got into, and Swahili. She never declared a major. In the jewelry class, she made necklaces for her girlfriends, and two silver bands for us. We made vows, an anti-marriage ceremony.

"With this ring, I thee dread," she said. I repeated the line, but I would've married her for real. Even though the rings were only jokes, I took mine seriously. I liked wearing it—it gave my thin fingers character, a weightiness I enjoyed. She wore the band for a while, but once the semester broke, she left hers on the nightstand. Next semester she was through with jewelry and on to something new—scuba diving, I think.

I've stocked up on all kinds of cleaning supplies: a broom, mop, bucket, Mr. Clean, Formula 409, Windex, Pine-Sol. I love all the colors—a chemical rainbow of solvents. The vibrant blue of Windex is best, like waters from an ancient Greek ocean. It cuts the film of the bathroom mirror, making my reflection clearer. I hate my face. I usually try to avoid mirrors and cameras. Celia's different. She looks better in pictures than in real life. Her face just burns off the paper. Every time I'm in a picture, my face widens, gets fuzzy edges. I ruined every picture we were in together, so I don't keep any of them out.

The whole place smells like a clean bathroom now. Even my toilet paper is scented. Celia scoffed if I bought it for the trailer. "I don't perfume that part of my body," she said.

"Seems to me that's where a person needs it most," I

said.

"You have a canine mentality." She always won.

Her parents tell me she's in Europe now. Even they don't know exactly where. They've received postcards from Florence, Hamburg, and Athens. Celia once told me that she wanted to swim every ocean in the world before she died. I imagine Celia swimming in those ancient oceans, never tiring, her skin blue in the water, gliding through the waves until she loses the shore and land forever.

After the bathroom, I start in on the kitchen. I rip out the shelf paper—a dark, fake wood grain—because roaches are known to lay their eggs underneath. What a place to be born—in glue, pinned under a utensil tray. Underneath the top layer is another, this time a pink graph design. I can tell there is one more layer underneath that. I could rip it all out, but instead take a craft knife and carefully slice off a corner. The bottom layer reveals a solid, avocado green. Matches my stove, original equipment from forty years ago. Those first owners must have really thought themselves stylish. I'll have to start over, with paper of my own, and hope the bugs don't take a liking to it.

When I move the stove to clean behind it, I send a family of lizards scurrying into a tiny hole in the baseboard. The guy I bought the house from warned me about them. He told me he let them stay because they eat the bugs. I can't catch them anyway, so I try to get used to their strange, prehistoric skin. I feel like I'm living among a colony of miniature dinosaurs.

Actually, I feel protective of the lizards. I'd hate it if they took my bumbling as an eviction notice. I suppose I felt the same way when Celia left—that, somehow, I'd driven her away. I'd been visiting my parents, and returned to a half-empty trailer and a check for two months' rent. Severance pay. Still, no matter how bitter I was—and I was—she put a fear in me that I could make what I loved disappear. Maybe I can make things work with the lizards.

With a sponge mop, I make a quick swipe of the kitchen tile, removing the grubby food stains. Judging from the evidence, the prospector's diet consisted entirely of pasta and red sauce, most of it never making it to a plate. I can see him shoveling the still-steaming noodles into his mouth, barely tasting the food before hurrying out the door to protect his claim. My role—cleaning up the mess of the adventurer—feels too familiar. I dispense with the mop and get down to hands and knees scrubbing. When I'm finished, all that's left are three bright orange globs, indelibly ground into the vinyl tile, refusing to be mined.

I met Celia at a friend's dorm party, a Bogart filmfest. She told me later that she was there by a fluke—she had been invited to a party on a different floor. "I stayed because you all looked so pathetic, smoking your cigarettes," she said.

So, coincidence became our theme. A running gag of "good things." Like, if I couldn't find my keys, I'd say, "Good thing I didn't find them—if we'd been on the road five minutes earlier, we would've had a wreck."

Hers were more elaborate. When we were too late for a movie she said, "Good thing we didn't see that movie. You would've been brainwashed by the Marxist subtext and organized a revolution that would've overthrown the government. Other world leaders, in a jealous rage over your spectacular goatee, would've resorted to nuclear weapons. We just saved the planet." Something like that.

My goatee was the only physical interest in me she ever admitted. I overheard her describing me on the phone as having a "sexy devil beard." She told me that a beard was the only thing she envied about a man. "It must be wonderful," she said. "To be able to grow a mask." I've since shaved mine.

Later, her version of coincidence grew obstructive, unsatisfied. "Good thing we went out tonight. Had I stayed in, a dark stranger would've come to my door, swept me off to Malta, and I'd have to spend the rest of my life on the beach." Or critical: "Good thing we drove your car. It just coughed up enough exhaust to shred the ozone a half-mile, giving another million Australians skin cancer."

My bathtub, choked with who knows what, will not drain. Showering in ankle-deep water because of someone else's hair clogs drives me nuts. Celia would shed hair all the time, but hers swirled into a feathery ringlet on top of the drain screen, easy enough to scoop away. This clog goes deep, so I buy Drano. It's powerful stuff, skull-and-crossbones type poison. Just picking up the bottle at the store makes me wash my hands as soon as I get home. I unscrew the cap. It opens scandalously easily. I pour half the bottle into the scummy water. With conscious intent, the yellow stream finds the hollow of the drain, deep through the recesses of God-knows-what dark, winding pipe bowels. In thirty minutes, the water is gone. True to its word. Calling a plumber is sacrilege—I'll believe in Drano.

When I hear a knock on the door as I'm fixing dinner, my mind races through a list: She hasn't had time to get back into the country; she doesn't have my address; she wouldn't feel obligated to knock. I hate how completely I know it isn't her. And I hate the disappointment I feel in spite of myself when I open the door. It's Bryan, the prospector.

"Sorry to bother you, but I think I left a gym bag here," he says.

"Haven't seen it," I say. "But you're welcome to look."

"If you wouldn't mind," he says.

I invite him in. "I won't be long," he says, and disappears into the bedroom. Foolishly, I wonder if he's left some sort of treasure. It would be just like me to have missed it.

He returns empty-handed. "No luck."

"You like beans and rice? I've just made dinner."

Bryan accepts, and sits at the table. "I hardly recognize the place."

"You're the first guest I've had," I say.

"It looks great. Sorry I left it such a mess," he says.

I consider asking him about the orange stains, but don't.

"It's weird," Bryan says. "Seeing someone else's things in your house."

"I haven't really settled in yet," I say, motioning toward the boxes stacked in the living room. I have the important things out: computer and table, TV, stereo, couch, loveseat, two bookcases with only half my books. A lone Monet print that I liked in the display plastic, but hate on my wall. I hate most of my stuff. If archaeologists dug up my house centuries later, who knows what they'd make of my life. Pieces to only half the puzzle. I probably should burn everything and start over.

I set two bowls on the table. "What would you like to drink?"

"Ice water is fine—I can't stay long."

I go to the cabinet and get down a plastic cup. The bottom and rim are stained brown. No matter how hard I tried, I couldn't get Celia to use glasses for the herbal tea she drank every night before bed. I put the cup in the sink and take down a glass.

"Find any gold yet?"

"Finding it's not the problem," he says, between bites. "We know it's there, and we know how to get it out."

This surprises me, since the trickiest part of archaeology is the excavation. I read a case where a guy thought he'd roped the dig site properly. He worked for three days trying to free a clay pot embedded in rock. It turned out to be an ordinary eighteenth-century item. When he got up, he found he'd been kneeling on a stone comb and pick from the Bronze Age, which he'd nearly crushed under his weight.

"What *is* the problem?"

"We need investors. Milling is expensive."

"So you won't be striking it rich?" I ask, disappointed. I'd hoped that someone was finding what they wanted.

"I didn't say that. We just need the money to get off the ground." He scrapes his bowl clean. "Interested in buying a share?"

A pitch for money. So, there was no gym bag. No hidden treasure. "No, I don't think it's for me." I lift the lid of the pot. "More beans?"

Bryan smiles. "I better be going. I have more people to see." At the door, he pauses. "I didn't think I'd ever miss this old house, but I do."

"Really?"

"I guess. Like leaving an old friend."

"I'll tell the lizards you say hi," I say, for levity.

"Lizards? Oh . . . right. Their cousins are living with me at the mine. Listen, think over the investment. It can't miss."

When he leaves, I fill the sink with dishwater. I take steel wool to the plastic cup. It's hard to get my hand into the cup, but I work and squeeze, scrubbing the bottom and lip of the cup, sweating into the dishwater, scratching away at the tea stains until the pad crumbles and I have to use my fingernails. But it's no use. I have to give up.

Celia's fingernails were a raw, bloody mess. She wore gloves at night to keep from biting her nails in her sleep. Her doctor said it probably wouldn't work, because most people would take the gloves off in their sleep. But she argued, "My subconscious is a wimp." And she was right—every morning they were still on. The first time she touched me in the morning, I thought I was being attacked by an ape.

Funny, I don't miss sleeping next to her. I sleep better without her. She squirmed in the night, like a child twisting from being tickled, or worse. When I got brave, I brought it up as a joke. "You sleep the sleep of the tormented," I said.

"You speak the speak of idiots," she said, and that was the end of it. She never seemed affected by the trials her body endured at night—she claimed she never slept better than when she slept next to me.

Now, I try to dream of her. She won't even come back then. I'll go to bed thinking of her, then lose her image to sleep. Until last night.

We're in an anthropology class together, and the professor—plump, middle-aged—loads a film about an African tribe's fertility ritual. The professor nibbles on a Hershey bar at his desk. The light flickers on the bare torsos of masked tribesmen, writhing to staccato drumbeats. Then, the professor sprawls out of his chair, his head turned to the right, his eyelids fluttering. I know he's having a stroke, but everyone in the room is frozen, including me. Except for Celia. She goes to him. Chocolate oozes from his mouth, pooling on the floor. Celia lifts his head, scoops the chocolate from his mouth, and performs CPR. The professor resuscitates, then takes Celia in his arms. She rubs his head and kisses him.

"Hey! What are you doing?" I say.

She lifts her head. "I'm saving his life," she says, her lips wet with chocolate.

This dream was no mystery. Nowhere, not even in my mind, will Celia be contained.

Before I can finish shaping up the house, I have to do something about the lawn. The overgrowth peeps in the windows, threatening to take over. Weeds are bursting everywhere. Gnarled leaves surround the tiniest of flowers. I can't tell the weeds from the good stuff. I'm scared to cut anything that's growing, so I hire a landscaping crew to do it for me.

After surrendering the outside, I concentrate on the inside. It seems I've stripped the years of dirt from the surfaces. Back to archaeological ground zero: now I can begin my own damage.

I spend half a day putting together a wooden filing cabinet, the first one I've ever owned. With the file, the bookcases, kitchen cabinets, and dresser drawers, I now have places for everything I own. But I can't finish. Once my old life is put away, I'll have to work on becoming a new person.

I'll have to be someone different. Celia knows what that's like, but I don't. Once, when we went hiking in the Arbuckle Mountains, we stopped to look at the falls. I dropped a quarter in the view finder for her. "This must be what it's like to be in someone else's head," she said. "Everything's distant, milky." She weaved back from the eyepiece, struggling to get her bearings. She's probably right—for those like her, who see the world clearly. When I took my turn, I could see just fine.

The day has come. I walk the house, searching for something to put away, to scrub. The kitchen sparkles. Floor, cabinets, oven, drip pans: all clean. The baseboards in the living room and halls glisten. My slippers squeak on the bathroom floor, the chrome in the tub winks back the light. Every book shelved, every paper filed. I have nothing left to do but *occupy*, which I realize I haven't done. The house isn't mine yet, and I know why. She hasn't seen it. All she has to do is see it. She'd come in, and say something like, "Look at you, all grown up in a house," and then it would be mine.

I flip through one of my books before going to bed, still feeling that the house isn't finished. I find a hair pressed between the pages and remember. She ran her hand through her hair every time she read. It's a long strand, though it seems shorter than her hair really was. I hold it between my fingers, stretch it across my wrist, down my arm. I put it to my nose and try to smell her shampoo, but there is nothing left. I close my eyes, get lightheaded. It feels like the house is trying to spin loose from its foundation. I think for a moment of riding that wave all the way back to Oklahoma, but that's the wrong way to go. The last I heard, they'd rediscovered oil there, and getting to it has caused the earth to shake in ways the land hasn't in many lifetimes. I know I'm still waiting for her, but I also realize that this one thin hair pinched between my fingers is the most I ever had, or ever will have, of Celia. I'm holding the one thing left in my house that needs my attention.

I hear the lizards rustle behind the stove, scrabbling for bugs. My home. Their home. I open my eyes.

I don't know what I'm going to do with this hair. If I keep it, Celia would make fun of me, and rightfully so. Too sentimental. I have to let it go. I could walk to the stove, drop the hair down as a gift to the lizards. She might think that was funny, ask me if I know anything about the nesting habits of reptiles. I do not. Ever since Celia left, I've been searching for alternate endings. One that might work out. Something that puts everything together so it makes sense. Celia was made only of beginnings, a river that knows one direction, never looking back. The one thing I do know about lizards is that they can shed their own tail. Sometimes the tail keeps moving after it's detached from the body. Why, I don't know. But I can guess.

I twist the hair back and forth in my hand. It comes

alive, for a moment. I decide that I will leave the hair for the lizards. As I watch the hair disappear into the dark behind the stove, I understand what was never mine, that discovering something does not make it mine. My hand hangs empty, fingers a little sore from holding on too tight, and it finally feels like everything is in its place.

Strong Black Hearts

Tyler knelt in the long grass beyond his grandfather's porch, fingers spread, flattening the grass into islands. He and his mother had come for a last vacation before he went back to school. They called it a vacation even though his grandfather lived only two hours away—still the farthest Tyler had been from home. Soon, Tyler would start the second grade, in a new classroom, but he tried not to think about that yet.

Tyler watched a bug creeping to his right hand. It had a dark gray shell, round like one of his little cars, but it had lines across it like they might be ribs, only on the outside. A shadow came over Tyler from behind. Tyler squinted up at the dark figure behind him. He tried to see his grandfather's mouth, but the words came from darkness.

"That's a roly-poly," his grandfather said. He wore an undershirt, the old kind without sleeves. Tyler's mom used to make him wear one too, until he started school. He told her that none of the other kids wore them, and that they called him a girl. She said it was okay, and he didn't have to wear them if he didn't want to. He hadn't since, but they were still tucked in his drawer next to his socks, folded in three sections, straps on top.

Tyler's grandfather knelt beside him, his hand on the back of Tyler's neck. "Pick it up," he said, revealing the false teeth that could pop out at any moment.

"It's dirty," Tyler said.

"It's all right." His teeth clacked. "Try and pick him up."

Tyler put his finger in front of the roly-poly, his hand bridging the grass to the back porch. It wiggled its antennae on the tip of his finger. They felt like the invisible hairs on his arms. Sometimes Tyler rubbed them and wondered if they would grow into the thick forest on his grandfather's arms. The roly-poly climbed on his finger, brushing its tiny legs up then down the back of his hand. Tyler smiled. "It tickles."

But his grandfather didn't smile.

"Darndest thing I ever saw. Here." He pinched the roly-poly between his finger and his long, yellowed thumbnail, then dropped it on the pavement. It curled into a ball and rolled to a stop.

"See?" His grandfather seemed pleased.

This reminded Tyler of another time with his grandfather. It was dusk, and Tyler had found the biggest worm he had ever seen—a wonderful monster with slime all over it, probably poisonous, definitely dirty. Tyler called for his grandfather, who came out with a glass salt shaker. His thumb bent as he carefully salted the worm. It collapsed on itself and dissolved, leaving Tyler staring at the damp spot in the soil.

Now, Tyler looked at the roly-poly, then at his grandfather. "Is he dead?"

"Naw, he's not dead. He's just protecting himself."

Tyler knew what that meant. "He's scared." Sometimes Tyler was afraid of his grandfather. His hair was short, a scrubby white flat-top. It looked like a vampire's. Tyler's mom called it a widow's peak. *Widow.* Tyler mouthed the word. When his first grade teacher had asked the class about their parents, some were divorced, but he was the only one who didn't have a father. His teacher called his mother a widow. He didn't like the way it sounded. Tyler had a widow's peak too, but his blond bangs covered it.

"Come on, boy. Let's take a walk." His grandfather went inside to put on a shirt and his hat. Tyler was glad he wouldn't have to look at his grandfather's hair.

Before they left, Tyler's mother stopped them in the doorway. "Look at those jeans."

Tyler looked at the knees, tinted with grass.

"Don't you think you should change?"

Tyler looked at his grandfather. "I like them like this."

His mother hesitated, then said, "I can't win against two of you." Usually, Tyler's mother acted like she could do anything, but not around his grandfather.

Outside, Tyler followed in deliberate footsteps. His grandfather was a different man in his hat—taller, stronger. Holding to his rough hand, Tyler felt how soft his own hand was, like his mother's.

The sun peeked over the brim of his grandfather's hat, and he glowed dark in the sun. Tyler looked at the sidewalk, measuring his grandfather's steps—two between each seam. Tyler took three steps to keep up.

He felt the pulse of his grandfather's blood through his hand to his own arm. Before Tyler was born, his grandfather had a heart attack. Only old people had heart attacks—his mom told him he shouldn't worry about having one. Normally, you die after a heart attack. The pills his grandfather takes are called nitroglycerin, like the stuff that explodes. His grandfather must be strong, swallowing tiny bombs.

A rumbling came from the sky and Tyler pointed up. "Look." A plane emerged from a cloud, trailing a silver plume. It banked right, then shot straight up. Tyler followed it until the sun got too bright. "My dad used to fly," Tyler said, his eyes closed, toward the sky.

"He was brave, your father. Real hero . . . " He never talked about Tyler's father. Tyler's mother said he didn't like to talk about people he loved who were gone. All Tyler knew about his father were stories his mother told. Those stories had just one picture—it hung in their hallway at home, a pale man in a cloth hat. His head was tilted, like he was thinking of a secret.

"Grandpa, were you afraid in the war?"

His grandfather stopped. "Son, you don't have to be afraid of anything."

Tyler nodded. He wanted to ask if his father died because he was afraid, but his grandfather was already talking about something else.

"Long as you stay in school, you don't have to worry. Don't, and you'll end up like your old grandpa."

"Where did you used to work?" Tyler had heard the story, but he liked it.

"Oil fields. Started fifty years ago. Worked roughnecks' hours—till the job was done."

"How much did you make?"

"Dollar a day. Sometimes had to wait a month for it, too."

Tyler couldn't imagine how they lived. A dollar didn't

buy anything.

"Your grandma would keep supper till dark. I'd sleep four hours, if I was lucky. Got to where I could feel the oil in my veins."

Tyler had seen pictures of his grandfather when he was younger. He was never smiling. Tyler wondered how his mother lived with such a man. Everything was black and white then—the houses, sky, grass, dirt, leaves. Everything was strong.

"You won't have to worry about that. You'll go to college. Be a lawyer or something, make a lot of money."

Tyler thought about the math and reading he did in school—easy compared to working in the oil fields all day. He already got five dollars a week allowance and didn't have to do anything. He'd never have to work in the oil fields. Tyler let his hand slip from his grandfather's. He thought about the strong black hearts that pumped the black blood through the men in photographs.

After dinner, Tyler played a game in the dining room while his grandfather and mother talked in the living room. Tyler could hear their conversation, but he pretended they were the enemy. Under the table, he was a prisoner of war, separated from his troops. The legs of the table and chairs were the prison's bars. He listened.

"Fine boy. Make a fine man."

"I'm just glad *you're* here for him," his mother said.

Tyler knew the enemy was talking in code. He'd have to break it if he wanted to escape.

"I'm glad I'm here myself."

"You just keep it that way." A change in tone. Was it fear?

He heard whispering, then his grandfather said, "In there? He's so quiet."

Everyone called him a quiet boy. He didn't know if this was good or not.

His mother said, "Come in here, Tyler. Say goodnight."

Tyler moved one of the chairs and came out. The game was over.

"There's Grandpa's little man." Tyler looked at the brown spots on his grandfather's hands and arms, all the way up to his undershirt strap. He looked small when he stretched out his arms. "C'mere and give the old man a hug."

Tyler closed his eyes as his cheek grazed the stubble on his grandfather's face.

"Night, Grandpa."

Tyler's mother took him to his room and tucked him in under his own bedspread they had brought from home. She thought it helped him sleep better. There were red and blue footballs on it, still visible in the dark. They weren't even brown, like footballs were supposed to be.

"You're really helping out with Grandpa's walks," she said. "He loves going out with you."

"Really?"

"Can't you tell?"

"I don't know."

"You should hear him. He's so proud of you. Did you know when you were born, he told all the nurses they shouldn't keep you with the other babies?"

"How come?"

"He said it would embarrass the other babies because they were so ugly."

Tyler smiled at this, but he thought he shouldn't.

She pushed his hair back and kissed his forehead. "Good night, son."

He lay awake, listening to the sounds from the living room. He wondered how his grandfather knew he was going to be a fine man. Like he could see pictures in the future, like what he did now didn't matter because later, when it really mattered, everything would be fine.

Tyler couldn't sleep, so he got up to get a drink of water. In the dark hallway, he paused in front of the pictures. His favorite was President Truman, shaking his grandfather's hand. Truman was short and smiled up at Tyler's grandfather, young and serious in his uniform. Next to that hung a framed pillow with a sewn-on purple heart and distinguished service medal. His father got a purple heart too, but it didn't do any good because he never got to see it.

Tyler walked to the bathroom and turned the faucet on quietly, trying not to wake his mother and grandfather. Hands cupped under the cool water, he sipped, went back to his room. When the smoke from his grandfather's cigarettes crept into the room, he put the covers over his head and curled to sleep in the heat of his own breath.

The next day, it was time to say goodbye. Instead of playing, Tyler straightened his room. "So it'll be ready for me," he said.

"Come here, boy. This place'll always be ready for you." Tyler expected a hug, but instead his grandfather put out his hand, and Tyler shook it. "Take care," he said.

Even though he didn't say what to take care of, Tyler knew it meant to take care of his mother. People told him that a lot, but his grandfather never had. "I will," he said, but like always, not knowing how.

Tyler's mother let him sit in the back seat and wave as the car drove away. He kept waving as his grandfather disappeared from sight, and kept waving for a long time after he knew there was no way his grandfather could see him.

In late October, several weeks into school, summer seemed far behind. Tyler had made new friends, and liked the second grade. He felt silly when he remembered how worried he was about it. But he already had his eye on the third graders, and wondered how hard the next year would be. He hadn't talked to his grandfather since, but Tyler thought of him often, and whenever he did he knew he still hadn't grown up, that he was still just playing.

Then at recess one day, a teacher interrupted his kickball game on the playground. His mother waited for him inside. She looked strange in the halls of his school— still and lonely. She told him what he'd always known could happen. His grandfather had died of a heart attack.

That night, he cried. "Didn't he take his pills?"

"Pills don't always work."

"But why did he have to die?"

"If he could have stayed with us forever, he would have. None of us can control that."

But Tyler knew that was wrong. His grandfather *had* controlled it last time, the time he had the other heart attack. His mother had said how strong he was, like it was his choice to recover. He stayed then, but not this time. What was different?

The night before the funeral, his mother told him what would happen. "Everyone will be at the church, just like Sunday. The preacher will talk about your grandpa."

Tyler twisted his foot in the carpet.

"The casket will be up front," she said.

"Will Grandpa be in it?"

"Just his body. When the preacher is done, they'll open the casket."

"So you can see him?"

"You don't have to. If you decide to go, you can pretend he's sleeping. And we can say goodbye."

"Did you get to say goodbye to Dad at his funeral?"

"In a way."

"But you couldn't see him, could you?"

"No, hon. You couldn't."

Tyler thought of his mother at his father's funeral, crying alone. He wished he could have been there. Then he remembered that his grandfather must have been there, to take care of her. After a moment Tyler said, "I want to go."

The family met at his grandfather's house before the funeral. There were people there Tyler had never met, some friends of his grandfather, some related. They weren't supposed to be in the house without his grandfather. Tyler stayed away, in the room that had been his on vacations.

Tyler's mother brought his clothes. "Time to get ready." She turned to leave.

"Wait, Mom. Did you bring an undershirt?"

"I didn't think you wanted one."

"It's okay."

After he dressed, he stood on a chair and got a box of cars, kept in the closet for him. Tyler played only with those his grandfather bought for him, dutifully running them across his shadow until they got so knotted up with the pale brown carpet fibers they wouldn't roll anymore.

With his grandfather gone, he felt like there was no top to the sky. The sun was bright and severe over his grandfather's church. It was older than Tyler's, no carpeting at all in the tiny auditorium. Inside, clumps of flowers circled the altar like peacocks standing guard. Yellow gladiolas towered over the reds, pinks, and purples of roses, carnations, and mums. The casket lay in front, closed, shiny and new.

He stood at the back with his mother. They had already seen everybody at the house, but his relatives came to shake his hand anyway. His great uncle took his hand firmly. His eyebrows, gray and bushy, covered his eyelids. "You being strong for your mother?"

"Yes," she answered for him. "He's my little man."

A tired-looking usher seated them near the front, then went to the altar and opened a half-door on the casket. The organ played slow music, and the usher motioned for their row to stand.

Tyler's mother whispered, "Are you all right?"

He nodded.

Tyler watched his feet. His shoes creaked against the wood floor. Some people cried, but he didn't look to see who. His mother stood over the casket first. She patted the side, her lips trembled, and she touched a handkerchief to her eye.

When she moved away, Tyler stepped to the altar. The

inside of the casket was all pillows and too smooth. Tyler stretched to see his grandfather's body. He looked white and small. Tyler had never seen his grandfather dressed up before, but now he wore a blue suit and tie. Tyler wondered if he was wearing an undershirt. His eyes were closed, but it didn't look like he was sleeping. He looked scared.

At his seat, Tyler closed his eyes like he was praying, but the picture he saw was his grandfather, the way he looked that summer. Tyler whispered, "I'm afraid, Grandpa."

They rode to the cemetery in a long line of black limousines. Tyler thought of them as giant roly-polies, tickling the road with their tires.

After the funeral, the family gathered at the house. Tyler stood in a corner of the dining room. The table was covered with a huge cloth, and lots of food. People held plates and glasses, laughed and talked, like it was Thanksgiving. One of his aunts caught him by the shoulder. "You better get some cookies before they're all gone."

He pulled away from her and slipped down the hall, to his grandfather's bedroom. He knew he must be quiet. In the doorway, his eyes adjusted to the dark. The hat hung by the door. Tyler put it on. He picked up the cigarette lighter, held his thumb tight, and breathed the whispering gas. His arm nudged the rocking chair, creaking against the hardwood floor. Tyler leaned against the standing ashtray next to the rocker and felt his heart beat against the rim, vibrating the stale ash. With his finger, he drew in the ash—dark eyes, hollowed cheeks, a strong chin. Not his father, or his grandfather, but himself. The self he and his mother would need if they were to make it alone. Staring at the ash smeared on his fingertips, he felt a darkness through him, nameless, the one that heated the black and white pictures of his young grandfather.

Wings

The night my father died, Mother dragged the mattress from his room, down the stairs and into the field, furrowing the dying grass. Moonlight skimmed the red streaks on her face as she tossed her head, her gray hair strung before her eyes. She turned the mattress, exposing the bloody impression on the ticking, damp and darkening in the icy air.

I watched, peeling bark from a sycamore tree. She gathered dry grass and sage and kindled a reluctant fire on the mattress. As the smoke drifted to the branches of the sycamore, the vapors of my breath rose and mingled with the smoke, and I imagined a fire burning in me. I never saw my father's body.

Mother slept with her head in the ashes. I went to her when the sun was still gray. The sleeve of her dress was tangled in the bristles of a vine. She awoke as I tried to release her.

She looked at me and with colorless lips tried to speak, but the languages had died. Her tears streaked the ash black on her cheek. She would never speak again.

The memories come to me as I work in my father's pumpkin field, where the children used to come. The pumpkins have no trouble growing in the sand the summer brings, but the other crops struggle. I should plow the patch and plant more sorghum, but I can't bear to grow anything else in that spot.

When Mother died, my brother and I took over the farm. We worked in the fields as children because Father was busy working on his clocks. Mother said you would think his clocks had souls. He said that every clock had its own magic. "Clocks don't create time. They listen, and show us."

The last clock he made was intended for me, but he never finished. He always had an adjustment to make. Many times it would tick and we would think it was working, but he would tear it apart and start over. He never said the problem was mechanical—only, "It cannot hear yet."

My father's pain touched my brother first, and then me. When my brother's pains became more frequent, he moved from the farm. I visit him often since we are the only family remaining. He tells me the pain still comes.

I have seen all the doctors. Some give me experimental medicines. The superstitious ones whisper about a family curse. I believe the pain will kill me, and I do not know why it waits.

My knees buckle to the ground. My neck arches and forces my ear to the earth. I feel a blossoming in my body. My vision clouds, but in the dust I see a flower, tongues of color I do not know. Of the questions I would ask my father, the answers would be in these colors.

Sometimes I dream I hear him breathing. An old man at the far edge of a lake reaches his hands toward me, sparks showering from his palms. They glide toward my eyes, reflecting in the lake. Then the sparks race, brighter, stinging orange salt in my eyes until I cannot see. I awaken to pain, but I hear nothing.

I remember Father at the Independence Day celebration by the river. I remember the low spark of fireworks, and the sting against my skin. From the top row of the grandstand, I looked to the dark sky. Father touched my arm, raised a clenched fist, then opened his hand. The sparks fell as if he released them and they burned to the river, floating the waves of air to the dark water, until I could see them only on the back of my closed eyes. The black river, my eyes.

If he would come to me now, it would be as he did when I was a child. He stood at the top of the stairs in his overcoat. The light of the moon shone through the window behind him, casting down the floor and onto the walls of our room the shadow of a great, flightless bird.

I have not seen my brother since last season. I bring him a pumpkin. When he answers the door, I notice a hunch in his shoulders, but the sight of the pumpkin cheers him, and he asks about the farm.

"Every day there is more sand."

He smiles. "Father would have said it comes from the stars."

Father spent his nights on the balcony, charting the stars with a small telescope. Once I asked what all the marks meant. He pointed my hand to the sky. He said the first clocks were made from the sun, and the calendars from the stars. They looked a muddle to me, but he said, "We can predict where they will move and what they will do. There is a pattern to the stars."

My brother says, "At one time, I thought Father could grow stars in the dirt."

When I was younger, I would have thought that possible. Now I am more practical. "I am leaving the farm."

My brother does not respond, though I can see his disappointment.

"I think the pain will cripple me . . . " but I stop before saying, *as it has you.*

"Do you remember the night he died?" he asks.

"I remember." We have discussed the night so often, our memories have become one. Every word, every sight we have memorized: I heard the susurrations of Mother's prayer language, buoying Father's cries. The sounds seemed to come not from him but from the door itself, deep in the grain of the wood.

"And you remember the dream you had that night?"

I have told him the dream many times. Father lay in his bed, his body swollen with pain, Mother slumped at his side. Then he let out a great cry. The side of his body split and unfolded huge black wings, slick with dark blood.

"Let me tell you what I've not told anyone," my brother says. "I had that same dream. I cannot be sure that it was only a dream."

My hands are shaking. My brother reaches out and holds them still.

176

My brother, like my father before him, will soon be gone. Then I will be alone. Tonight I lie in bed. Though I have worked in the sun all season, my skin has not browned. My shoulders are red with burn. I scratch and my nails loosen thin, white strips. I look to the mantel, where my father's clock sits, hands unmoving. I keep it, hoping someday I may learn to make it work.

The fan lulls me toward sleep, and I hear the breathing. The man on the other side of the lake throws the sparks, but I catch them on the back of my eyes, melting them as if they were snowflakes. I feel the touch of my father, as if wings are inside me. He reaches his hands to me, and I see tender pink scars under his arms. My tongue seizes, and all I say is, "The pain."

I hear him speak in the darkness. "Take more."

And then, as he reaches toward me, his mouth moves but I hear the voice of Mother. "Listen for the brush of your wings."

He is gone, and I look to the window. The moon is a silent orange, as if a pumpkin has risen from the sand and ascended the night. Something that can't be spoken is happening, inside all of us.

The clock on the mantle moves forward a tick.

Body

As the odor of the anatomy lab throbs in Owen's sinuses, he wonders if there might be life in the room after all, if the spirit of the six cadavers might enter his body. Owen's first semester in medical school half over, the eight weeks of tugging, slicing and carving have degraded the bodies into holiday leftovers, viciously plucked prehistoric birds. Face-down for easier access to the spinal cord, they are not human—the instructor made that clear the first day when she called them "specimens." The smell, Owen knows, comes from a preservative the lab assistants spray on the bodies: a mixture of water, phenyl oxyethanol, and propylene glycol, the latter a holding component in hairspray, among other uses.

Medical school has been his parents' dream, not Owen's. They used to pencil in *Doctor* in his scrapbook under its yearly prompt: *What I want to be.* But Owen had secretly wanted to be a detective—at the scene of the crime, looking for clues, sifting evidence. He would search for killers in fingerprints, fibers, hair samples, his gloved hands scraping blood samples with a knife into a plastic bag. He would label the bags and take them to the lab—forensics, ballistics—where the puzzle would be shaped into truth.

True, most of these ideas were based on television mysteries he watched with his best friend. Cross and he had often been mistaken for brothers, and vowed never to be separated. Owen last spoke with him two years ago, a strained phone conversation. Owen sees even the childhood differences now—Cross liked the courtroom, but Owen was more impressed with the science of the crime than the Perry Mason tactics. He knows now, and probably sensed it then, that exacting the confession is easy. We all want our ugliest parts laid open, displayed for approval.

Now Owen works as a detective, investigating his life. His gut tells him that a murder has occurred, but he can't find the body. He feels only a vacancy that once must have contained his essence, a purpose. In its place he feels only a squeeze in his throat.

The instructor diagrams the spinal cord on the blackboard, and Owen follows on his cadaver, his gloved finger tracing the cord to the neck, where it is neatly cut at the base of the brain. The cranium is empty, wired shut like a marionette, the brain removed for Neuroanatomy, second-semester. The instructor distinguishes the regions of the spinal cord by color: cauda equina, blue; conus medullaris, yellow; dorsal rootlets, orange. Owen's cadaver, a large male with a catheter still in place, is one color, grayish-brown. Before the class, Owen had half-expected the bodies to slosh the bright red of video heart surgery—but the color is as quiet as the slightly parted lips.

When class is over, the lab assistants spray the cadavers, which lie in thin metal coffins called tanks. When the tanks are open, Owen remembers a documentary where a doctor tried to prove the existence of the soul. Dying people came to his lab and slept on giant meat scales while the cameras rolled. When the point of death came, the needles on the scales fluttered. Apparently, the soul weighs three ounces.

The assistants zip up the milky vinyl body bags. The seams surrounding the zippers have detached in several places, leaving gaping windows. Bits of flesh have collected in the folds of the catheter man's bag, and Owen sees a chunk fall to the floor as the assistant cranks down the platform of the tank. The floor has two large drains, so Owen assumes that janitors wash down the lab with disinfectant. Even so, the floor retains a slickish gummy texture that clings to the bottom of his sneakers.

Owen emerges from the chilled air of the basement into the Kansas night—cool, but warmer than the lab. Light from other campus buildings dots the sky. Owen imagines the world outside the lab as an anonymous audience in a darkened theater, straining to see. Some of the students opted for the daytime class because they said meeting at night was spooky, but Owen likes the intimacy. His hands tingle with the breaking of taboo.

At his apartment, the red light on his answering machine winks. "Hey, it's Gary. Why'd you leave so fast? A bunch of us are getting together at Fuzzy's. Close up the books." Owen had planned to catch up on his studies, but after the anatomy lab, he thinks it might be nice to be around some life, even if it is the boozy crowd at Fuzzy's.

He finds Gary sitting with the other first-year guys, an enclave of bachelors in their otherwise mostly-married or seriously-involved class. Owen is a few drinks behind.

"O-Man!" Gary says, pronouncing it as if he were a super-hip Rasta-man. "We're keeping one warm for you."

Owen sits, orders a beer, and watches the others make their plays. Owen had met a girl named Shannan here, but it didn't go well. She was quick-witted and pretty, but when he brought her back to his apartment, her perfume triggered the memory of the smell of the lab preservative. He could barely kiss her. Those first weeks, he smelled the lab everywhere—on new leather, the Scotchguard on his boots, the polyurethane on his windbreaker, and, because of the latex on the gloves, his hands. He made an excuse about an early Saturday class to get Shannan to leave.

Owen finishes his beer alone, the others away on "patrol." He has almost decided to leave when Gary appears with a platinum blond. "O-Man, this is Sylvia. I told her you could take care of her." Gary shoots him a pleading look, which Owen supposes means that Gary's about to score with Sylvia's friend.

"Have a seat," he says, as a favor to Gary, even though he doesn't feel like he owes him. Gary orders two beers, slaps the table, and spins back onto the dance floor.

Fuzzy's is a well-known med-school hangout—nobody's motives for hooking up can be fully trusted. Owen is suspicious of Sylvia's game, her tanning bed skin and gold signet rings on every finger. She's likely sizing him up for her investment portfolio. Gary likes to play up the sugar-daddy persona, telling the women he's farther along in school than he is, closer to financial maturity.

The beers come, Budweiser in bottles, and Sylvia asks Owen: does he want to "kick it?"

He hesitates before realizing she is asking him to dance, then says, "That would be fine." He leaves his beer on the table, but Sylvia dances with hers in hand.

The high, jerky disco tones drown out Sylvia's voice, so she puts her arms on his shoulders and talks past his ear. "Where you from?"

Owen shouts toward her nose, "Oklahoma."

He can't tell if she hears him, but she takes a sip from her beer, which he takes as a sign that it's okay to be from Oklahoma. Sylvia sways her head from side to side as she dances, fluttering her eyes as if she doesn't want to look at Owen's face. Her eyelashes spread like antennae, as if each one has been individually primped. Owen imagines her routine: reclined, head back, covered with worker ants lovingly grooming their queen.

"I think it's great what you do," Sylvia says to his ear.

"What?" Owen knows she can't mean his dancing. His movements, all arms and legs, left then right, look not like dancing but like he can't make up his mind which direction to run.

"Your friend told me you're a doctor," she says.

"No," Owen says, about to tell her he's a student, but suddenly says, "I sell insurance."

Sylvia glides back, puts the bottle to her lips, and upside-downs what's left, at least half the bottle, in one breath. For the first time, she looks him in the eye. She wiggles the bottle. "My beer's empty," she says, and melts into the crowd.

On his way home, Owen wonders why he said insurance—his father's profession. His father had wanted to be a doctor himself, but his family didn't have the money. Owen thinks his medical degree might pay back his parents for the life they never had. Like a baby learning to crawl, exploring the world on his hands and knees, turning back every now and then to make sure he hasn't lost sight of his parents, he searches for himself, but he finds only a pull from his youth, as if his center is attached by bungee cord to a big cement block in Oklahoma. The farther he goes, the more likely he'll snap back home.

Owen spends Saturday at the library preparing for a Histology exam and Monday night's lab on the vertebrae. No surprise that none of the Fuzzy's crowd is there; two of the guys have stopped going to classes altogether and will probably be out at the end of the semester. He studies through lunch, and only when the people at the neighboring tables begin staring does he notice his growling stomach. His watch reads 4:50—he wonders why his body has stopped registering time.

At his apartment, he fixes a Budget Gourmet dinner, and thinks *if Sylvia could see me now.* Gary calls, interrupting dinner. "O-Man, what's the idea leaving me stranded like that? She not pretty enough for you?"

"It wasn't that . . . "

"No problem. Didn't slow me down. Listen, you up for it again?"

"Geez, man. Don't you guys ever study? Count me out."

Owen is annoyed by Gary. Unlike his dropout buddies, Gary will make it—with virtually no effort. Gary's reckless charm lands him on his feet, but Owen can't afford to give up his responsibilities.

In the middle of his studies, the phone rings—the weekly call from his mother. "How's my doctor?" she says.

"Fine, Mom." There are long silences when they talk. He can feel her trying to understand him through the silence. He would like for her to talk away his problems as if he were a child, but he doesn't know how to tell her what they are.

When he was twelve, he would look in the mirror and try to imagine his adult face. Would he be handsome? A movie star? Would he ever really be adult? The mirror's cloudy reflection softened and flattered. Owen stood inches from it, squinted, and saw a fully-grown man, his future self. He had been comforted, as if he understood God's plan. Now, he feels he has betrayed that twelve-year-old's vision. Then, satisfaction came easily, throwing a football at recess. Since then, the cells in his body have regenerated completely, at least three times.

His mother asks him if he's going to church in the morning. She calls Saturday, not Sunday morning, so her question will be a suggestion, not a demand. Owen has stopped going to church, another betrayal, but he doesn't explain. Instead, he gives the same answer. "I might."

That night, Owen sits in front of the television, holding a fork, eating pineapple rings from the can. In high school, Saturday night was big. In Cross' Jeep, they cruised Main, until it emptied and the traffic light's message changed, aimed only at them: caution, caution.

They sometimes drove to the one-strip airport outside of town, where Cross' dad kept a plane. Cross was training for his pilot's license. But Owen was afraid—not just of flying, but of the enormity of the planes themselves, especially at night. He never stayed at an airport motel because of the noise, the roar of a metal monster borne from a seam in the sky, chilling the muscles in Owen's neck and bending him in fear.

Even after Owen told Cross his fear, they drove the

runway. Cross said it was the only place to run the quarter mile, but Owen knew the runway meant more. Cross needed the release, or he wanted Owen to overcome his fear—either way, Owen was doing Cross a favor.

Cross lost a lot of rubber, but he always stopped short of the barbed wire fence just beyond the runway. Owen never felt the excitement that Cross felt, just a sense of danger that could come suddenly, unseen.

Owen puts the can to his lips, his tongue grazing jags of metal, and drinks the tin-flavored juice. He pulls back the curtain and looks at the other apartments. His is the only light on.

Before going to bed, Owen makes one last pass in his lab manual. Then he pulls out his blood pressure kit from his nightstand. He's been keeping track, for practice—103 over 70, the range it has been for a month with only slight fluctuation. He holds the dial of the stethoscope to his chest. His mother had rheumatic fever when she was a baby and kept a stethoscope ever since, so she could monitor her own heartbeat. Owen had thought it was a toy, and wanted to listen to his chest, too. His heartbeat frightened him. How could life squeeze from his chest? Now, he tries to discern a message in the thump-thump, the bass notes of first music—the body's rhythm.

Owen wakes earlier than usual Sunday morning and wonders if this is a sign that he should go to church. He's willing to believe in signs—if not spiritual, then physiological. He has always envied the people who open the Bible randomly and find comfort. He opens his Bible: Psalms 73:27. "For, lo, they that are far from thee shall perish: thou hast destroyed all them that go a whoring from thee." He can't help but smile at the juxtaposition of sex and God. This passage seems like it could be speaking to him, but is enough off the mark to leave the message uncertain. He decides to go to church.

Gravel in the church parking lot powders his shoes. As Owen crouches to brush off the dust, a heavy-set usher leans over him. Owen shakes hands with him, a thick-fingered man who calls him brother. Owen is reminded of his father's feelings about the pressing of flesh. "Either religion is your politics, or politics is your religion." But the lines aren't so clear for Owen—either option suggests a system that can be believed in.

Organ music drifts into the lobby, and as Owen takes a seat in the middle of the sanctuary he hears the reverberation of drums. When did they get drums in church? Owen is sorry he came. The song leader can't stop smiling as he sings from transparencies projected onto the wall. The hymnals sit in their slots, unused. Owen picks one up and thumbs through the pages of the old songs while the rest of the congregation sings—choruses with all mention of sin edited out.

The minister is a missionary from a country in Africa. Owen is afraid the man will use words like "savages" and "heathens," but he does not. Owen tries to dislike him, but he can't. He reminds Owen of the boys he grew up with in high school. His face belongs on the side of a can of biscuits—tall, Hungry-Jack good looks, his shoulders rolling in a tightly-seamed jacket.

He asks for money with one hand fisted around the microphone, the other reaching up, down, like a boxer. The organ murmurs an alleluia chorus as he weaves in front. Then, the minister reaches out to Owen. He feels singled out, accused. Until he sees the man's eyes. Clouded, teary, they don't seem to penetrate the physical world, the solidity of the bodies standing before him. He smiles, as if his soul is already dancing in heaven. Owen takes a five dollar bill from his wallet, drops it in the offering, and leaves during the altar call.

Owen spends Monday in Biochemistry and Physiology classrooms, then Gross Anatomy. During the short dinner break between lecture and lab, Owen reviews his notes on the vertebrae and pelvis. Though he spent the weekend memorizing, the names of the tiny bones assault him like names of his ancestors, inhabitants of his subconscious. New information slips easily away. Is he running out of room?

Minutes before lab is to begin, the phone rings. Owen picks up the receiver expecting Gary, asking for notes. Instead, he hears the small voice of someone he knows he should recognize. The voice travels through his body, searching for a space.

"Owen? It's Cross."

He says he knows it's been a couple of years, but he knew Owen would want to know. Cross' father had been "losing touch." Cross and his two sisters had been taking turns living with him. He went for drives and got lost. The police knew him, and brought him home. Once, when they found him sitting in a field, he told the police to get out of his house. The family took away his car keys, but he had another set. They found his car half-submerged in the lake south of town, door open, engine running. He must have thought he was walking up the drive to his house.

"I thought you should know," he says.

"I'm sorry," Owen says. "I have to go to class. I have to . . . I'm sorry."

The fluorescent lighting in the lab radiates barely perceptible dead spots on the cadavers. The bulb buzzes. His cadaver tonight has petechial spots dotting her thoracic region, a telltale sign of asphyxiation by drowning, the same spots that would have formed in Cross' father, deprived of oxygen, the serous membrane erupted into pinprick bruises.

Owen rarely is forced to consider that the cadavers' utilitarian function is preceded by life. Cadavers reveal little about their relationships. Students know only the cause of death. Purportedly, a funeral has already been held, with cremation to follow. Owen cannot reconcile these bodies with life—when he does imagine their lives he thinks of them as walking dead, every movement anticipating the groping hands of amateur healers.

Death is not instantaneous.

Coroners do classify some deaths as sudden, but more often than not, any pronouncement of exact cause is fiction. Even more so the time of death—body tissue simply doesn't die simultaneously. The organs keep working. The brain may die, the heart may stop, but the body retains momentum. Owen wonders if the cadavers are still struggling, if decomposition is motion toward a goal as blind as the body's in life.

Every tank opened, the odor covers his skin. The chemicals glaze his body. His joints stiffen, the lights make him dizzy. He steadies himself against the back table, where plastic models of the four classifications of vertebrae are displayed. He looks for the familiar articulation of bone, but sees such a slight change in each vertebrae, the last thoracic is almost indistinguishable from the first lumbar vertebra. Relativity is the key—you have to see them together.

The lab assistant's gloved hands move with rough jerks as she berates the students for being delicate. "You have to dig in." Owen watches as Gary fumbles with a section of skin too thick with bubbled yellow fat to fold back. He cuts it off for a better view and drops it in an orange wastebasket marked "Anatomical Waste Only!" Every day the cadavers lose skin, flesh, fat, become lighter in their tanks, closer to their end, which Owen imagines is a center—pithy, spiritual—or nothingness. Owen suspects they are losing more than what he cuts out; maybe even looking diminishes them.

Finished with his incision, Gary turns up the volume on his headphones, stands over the tank, and uses his gloved knuckles as drumsticks. He sways his head back and forth, laying out a steady, metallic beat on the fingerprint-smeared lid. Owen's stomach turns as Gary's pounding grows insistent, personal, as if it were meant only for Owen. Gary's body convulses, his eyes flutter, his arms move like pistons as he reaches the finale: a flurry of a soft roll, three hard beats, then a savage thrust in the direction of the asphyxiated woman's head. *Pssh,* Gary imitates the cymbal, the sound of air escaping from a fire. Owen puts his hands over his ears and hurries from the building.

The fresh air soon settles his stomach, and he checks his watch. 7:12. If he doesn't stop, he can make it to Cross' doorstep by 2 AM. Leaving will jeopardize his standing in class, maybe even in school, but right now, the pull is strong and certain. He drives with the urgency he felt as a child, running home in the dying light.

Owen opens the vent to let in the cool evening air. He breathes slowly until the dizziness subsides. As the sky darkens, the moon lowers, centering over Oklahoma, his destination. Owen sees the gray upside-down rabbit in the moon, a detail he learned in Astronomy. Owen shakes his head—it took a university course for him to be able to see a rabbit in the moon.

Owen hasn't seen Cross in two years; he knows Cross has a son only a few months old. Owen has changed himself, surely, but there's no one to make a judgment. Like when you're a child, and you would grow, those closest can't tell. It's too gradual. Forces move, inside and out, slowly, imperceptibly. Will he be recognized? Owen drives toward the moon as if it were a target, a luminescent, inevitable bulls-eye.

Owen pulls into Cross' driveway at 1:57, the same driveway Owen pulled into almost every night of high school—the launching pad for the night's activities. The house is dark. Owen tries a soft knock. He wonders if he should go to his parents' house, and come back in the morning. But the moment he is searching for might be gone by then. He knocks louder. Owen hears shuffling inside, and the door opens to Cross, squinting. Nothing about him has changed, but he looks more intense, his features bolder.

"You lost?" he asks.

"I don't think so," Owen answers. He opens his arms, and Cross steps into the embrace. It occurs to Owen that they have never touched, no more than a handshake. The moment feels unearned, not a sharing of comfort but a greeting card.

Owen pulls away. "I didn't come for this, you know."

"No," Cross smiles. "I didn't think so."

"You still have the Jeep?"

"In the garage."

In Cross' Jeep, the plastic top flutters. They take old 66, the tires pulsing, thump thump over the concrete seams. At the airport, they circle the hangar where Cross' father kept his single-engine Cessna. Cross stops the Jeep at the end of the runway. "You ready?" Cross asks, as if the ride is all for Owen.

Owen sits back. "Let's go."

Cross pulls out slowly, gathering speed. The pebbles grind. Owen sees only pavement and wheat fields. The moon lights his spine. The Jeep jumps quickly into third, fourth, and settles in fifth. The wind pulls Owen's hair back, dries his eyes. The night swirls around him, his lungs burning, the air too fast. Cross' mouth spreads to a grin as he lets out an inhuman howl. Owen clutches his seat. He doesn't look at the speedometer, but he knows it is fast. At the end of the runway, the barbed wire fence comes into view, and Owen raises his arms and in that moment feels like two people, one watching the other as it lurches and groans, struggling to lose the pavement, grasping for that perpendicular shaft of lift, to catch that shelf of air and lose all weight in an instant.

Acknowledgments

Certain works in this collection have been previously published in *Arts & Letters* ("Moths," 2013); *Cincinnati Review miCRo* ("The Griefbearer," 2018); *Confrontation* ("Sitcom Mom," 2012); *Hawai'i Review* ("The Lucky Ones," 1995, which was reprinted in *Best Texas Writing*, 1998); *7 Artists, 7 Rings—an Artist's Game of Telephone* for the *Huffington Post* ("The Spooky House" (as "Glow of the Wick"), 2011); *Hunger Mountain* ("Triumph, Only Triumph," 2010); *Kenyon Review Online* ("The Marks," 2019); *The Massachusetts Review* ("Body," 1997); *New Orleans Review* ("The Girl With One Arm," 2010); *Phoebe* ("Cleaning House," 2003); *Press* ("The Baptist," 1997); *RE:AL* ("Strong Black Hearts," 2000); *Threepenny Review* ("Assisted Living," 2000, which was reprinted in *The World is a Text*, Prentice Hall, 2003); *Washington Square* ("Wings," 2005).

Thanks to my family: My mom, who made everything a story. My dad, who really wanted to know what happens at the end of "The Baptist." My wife Alecia, first reader, best reader. My children Isaac and Charlotte, and their beautiful indifference about everything in these pages.

Thanks to my brother Scott, and all of our Hardy Boys books. Thanks to the editors of publications these stories appeared in, particularly: Wendy Lesser, Chris Chambers, Brian Clements, Allen Gee, Nicole Walker, Caitlin Horrocks, Jonathan Silverman. Thanks to Jim Byl, without whom the story "Moths" wouldn't have been written. Thanks to these trusted readers: Dean Rader, Nancy Pennington, Oindrila Mukherjee, Mike Salisbury. Thanks to my junior high and high school teachers, especially: Robert Lea, Vauda Horak, Brenda Lumpkin. Thanks to my workshop teachers: Tom Lorenz, Carolyn Doty, Debra Monroe, Tom Grimes, Miles Wilson, Daniel Stern, Chitra Divakaruni, Kathleen Cambor. Thanks to the April poetry group where I sneaked in some flash fiction: Todd Kaneko, Amorak Huey, Amy McInnis, Aaron Brossiet, Gale Thompson. Thanks to these Kansas friends: Bill Kueser and the Munchers Bakery crowd, Karl Woelz, Christy Prahl, Tess Callahan. Thanks to these Southwest Texas friends: Darren Defrain, Kevin Grauke, Scott Blackwood, Jeff Utzinger, Greg Oaks. Thanks to these Houston friends: Averill Curdy, Naeem Murr, Marty Lopez. Thanks to my Grand Valley State University colleagues past and present, especially those who offered me a job doing what I love, including: Patricia Clark, Mark Schaub, Ellen Schendel, Dan Royer, Roger Gilles. Thanks to Dawn Nagelkirk who makes everything easier. Thanks also to Ellen, Patrick Johnson, and Lisa Gullo for the Writing Retreats and all the M&Ms. Thanks to all of my students at Grand Valley State University, for challenging me to be a better reader and writer. Finally, thanks to all of you reading this. These stories are for you.

About the Author

CHRIS HAVEN was born in Oklahoma, the son of a grocer and a storyteller. *Nesting Habits of Flightless Birds* is his first book. In addition to his short fiction work, a collection of poems, *Bone Seeker*, is forthcoming from NYQ Books; further poems can be found in *The Southern Review*, *Cincinnati Review*, *Pleiades*, *Mid-American Review*, and *Beloit Poetry Journal*, and prose poems from his Terrible Emmanuel series have appeared in *Denver Quarterly*, *Sycamore Review*, *North America Review*, and *Seneca Review*, where they won the Deborah Tall Award for Lyric Essay. He has degrees in Creative Writing from the University of Kansas, Texas State University, and the University of Houston. He lives with his family in Grand Rapids, Michigan, where he teaches courses in writing and style at Grand Valley State University.

CPSIA information can be obtained
at www.ICGtesting.com
Printed in the USA
JSHW010842111120
9499JS00001B/18